Hi there,

I just wanted to say hello and tell you a bit about myself.

I live on the very outside of London near the River Thames, with my husband (who is Dutch and makes great pancakes!) and our two young daughters. We also have a Siamese cat called Hamish who came to us as a very timid rescue cat and spent the first few weeks hiding up the chimney! Now he is a real family cat and loves sitting on my lap (and trying to sit on my keyboard!) when I'm at my desk writing.

I'm half Welsh and half English but I grew up in Scotland. Before I became a writer I worked as a doctor, mainly with children and teenagers. From as far back as I can remember I've always loved stories in any form – reading books, watching films, playing make-believe games. As a child I always had one fantasy world or another on the go and as I grew older that changed to actual ongoing sagas that I wrote down in exercise books and worked on for weeks at a time.

I really hope you enjoy reading this – and that you'll write to me at Gwyneth.Rees@bloomsbury.com to let me know what you think. I'd love it if you told me a bit about yourself too!

Best wishes,

Gwyneth

Books by
GWYNETH REES

LIBBY
in the
Middle

GWYNETH REES

BLOOMSBURY

LONDON OXFORD NEW YORK NEW DELHI SYDNEY

Bloomsbury Publishing, London, Oxford, New York, New Delhi and Sydney

First published in Great Britain in August 2017 by Bloomsbury Publishing Plc
50 Bedford Square, London WC1B 3DP

www.bloomsbury.com

BLOOMSBURY is a registered trademark of Bloomsbury Publishing Plc

A CIP catalogue record for this book is available from the British Library

ISBN 978 1 4088 5277 4

Typeset by RefineCatch Limited, Bungay, Suffolk
Printed and bound in Great Britain by CPI Group (UK) Ltd, Croydon CR0 4YY

1 3 5 7 9 10 8 6 4 2

For Philippa Lawrence-Chan

Chapter One

'Well, I don't see any dead bodies lying around, Dad,' I joked as we drove away from our old house for the final time.

Dad acted like he hadn't heard. Either he was too stressed to bother even trying to get my joke or he honestly didn't remember saying, 'Over my dead body!' when the idea of moving to live near Aunt Thecla had first come up. Aunt Thecla is Dad's totally interfering older sister. She's always lived in the same village where the two of them grew up, and she and Dad have never got on. Dad has always said he couldn't wait to get away from that village, though Mum says she's sure he exaggerates when he tells us stories about how awful it was to grow up there.

After a lot of persuasion Mum had finally talked him round, and for the last couple of weeks he had tried to be positive about it, at least in front of my sisters and me. We all knew that having Aunt Thecla living on our doorstep wasn't going to be easy. She's such a busybody, always sticking her nose in and dishing out her opinions on everything and everybody. Mum says our aunt's own life can't be that fulfilling if she has to take such a huge interest in other people's, but Dad says that's no excuse. Plus he says she's rich enough to take up loads of hobbies and go on lots of exciting holidays whenever she gets bored.

'She's bribing us to get what she wants,' Dad had warned Mum when Aunt Thecla had first made her unbelievable offer.

'So what if she is?' Mum said. 'She's clearly doing this because she's lonely after losing Hughie, but in any case she's doing us a huge favour. I mean, I know she's loaded, but three sets of private school fees is no mean offering.' (Hughie was our aunt's dog, and she was devastated when he escaped from her garden recently and got run over.)

'I'm telling you, Nina,' Dad persisted, 'you don't know my family like I do. She might not be like my father and make us repay her in blood and spit, but she'll have her own agenda, you can be sure about that! This is all about her being in charge of us.'

'Oh, Paul! If this is about what happened when you were a boy, then quite frankly I think it's time you forgave her.'

'I *have* forgiven her!'

'*Consciously* maybe.'

'I thought you were a dentist, not a psychiatrist,' Dad snapped.

'Forgiven Aunt Thecla for *what*?' I'd interrupted, but that just made them both cross with *me* for listening in. I have to admit that I do listen in to other people's discussions quite a bit. Mum says that I'm far and away the most curious one in our family, and I guess that's true.

I'd forgotten all about that conversation while we prepared to leave. I was far too busy saying my last goodbyes to various friends and to our old house and neighbourhood. I found myself feeling unexpectedly sentimental about things I'd hardly noticed on a daily basis – the blue garden gate I'd help Dad paint one summer, the park at the bottom of our road where I'd learnt to ride a bike, the big oak tree I always passed on the way to school, and our corner shop, which was the first shop I'd been allowed to walk to all on my own back when I was seven. Then there was Luke, our friendly window-cleaner, and Jovanka, our cleaning lady, who cried and gave us sweets on the day she said goodbye. I'd already said goodbye to most people I knew from school when we'd all broken up for the summer holiday.

It had been weird how suddenly lots of people at school who I'd never thought particularly liked me came up to give me hugs on the last day. I suppose I've always been one of the quiet ones at school, and since my best friend, Sarah, moved away I'd always felt a little bit of an outsider there. It was strange to receive all this positive attention from people who I thought barely noticed me, and to suddenly feel like a part of my school just as I was leaving. Even though I'd only been there for a year (I was just finishing Year Seven), a lot of teachers said they'd miss me and made a point of wishing me well. I had a feeling some of them felt sorry for me being uprooted, especially as I'm not exactly the sort of person to burst confidently into a new school and effortlessly make new friends.

At home I was doing my best to keep clear of the frequent tantrums of my almost-sixteen-year-old sister, Bella. This move was not what she wanted either, because it meant leaving behind her boyfriend, Sam. Sam has just turned seventeen (too old for Bella, according to Dad), and a few months earlier he'd dropped out of school. The fact that he'd immediately started an apprenticeship at his uncle's garage had stopped Dad being too scathing about that, but in any case my parents weren't exactly heartbroken to be taking Bella away from him.

Now that we were all crammed together in our car, I could sense my whole family was really close to meltdown. As usual, I was stuck in the middle between Bella and our six-year-old sister, Grace. Bella and Grace look like sisters, whereas I always think I look like the odd one out. They both have dainty features, pale complexions with rosy cheeks, and glossy dark-brown straight hair and large brown eyes. I've got grey-blue eyes, loads of freckles and thick curly reddish-brown hair that comes down to my shoulders. And there's absolutely nothing dainty about me.

'Move over, Libby,' Bella snapped as we left our street behind. A few years ago she wouldn't have cared if we were squashed together with our thighs touching, or even if I'd been perched on her lap, but now she acts like any physical contact between us has to be avoided at all costs. She calls it an invasion of her personal space.

'I can't! I've got Grace's seat digging into me on this side!' I protested.

'You can move your leg away from mine!'

'Girls, will you please stop squabbling,' Mum said crossly.

'We're not!' Bella retorted. 'We're having a *discussion* about who's taking up the most room. Which is definitely Libby!'

I didn't stand up for myself. I knew if I tried to challenge her she'd start spouting hard facts about the size of my bum in relation to hers. Although she's three years older than me she's really slight in build, like Mum and Grace. I'm the only one who takes after Dad's side of the family in that I'm 'a good healthy size', as Aunt Thecla would put it. Aunt Thecla isn't fat but she's definitely pretty solid, and you'd probably take me for her daughter rather than Mum's if we were all standing together.

Aunt Thecla had been visiting us once or twice a year for as far back as I can remember, and she always made a big thing of scrutinising our appearance, commenting on all the ways my sisters and I had changed. Not only was she like most adults who'd say, 'Look how much you've grown!' she wouldn't actually leave it at that. She always stared at us for so long it made us really uncomfortable, and then insisted on pointing out her various observations like, 'Libby's shoulders are so broad now – just like Mother's ...' and 'Bella has exceptionally big toes – she gets those from her grandfather' and 'You've got your grandfather's legs, Libby – but hopefully there's more they can do these days for varicose veins …'.

Needless to say she annoyed us all no end.

'I hate this stupid car, Dad!' Bella complained loudly. 'I don't know why we can't get one like Sam's mum's, with those pop-up seats in the back.'

'Pop-up seats in the crumple zone, you mean!' Dad said. 'I've seen her car. Those seats are a deathtrap.'

'What's a deathtrap, Daddy?' Grace asked with a frown. 'Is it dangerous?'

Bella sent her a withering look. 'Well, what do *you* think?'

'It's nothing for you to worry about, darling,' Mum said swiftly, 'though I must say I can't see why she even needs such a big car when it's just the two of them.'

'Sam's uncle was getting rid of it,' I told her.

Bella, who continued to glare daggers at the back of Dad's head, snapped, 'I don't think Sam's mum would make him sit there if it was a *deathtrap*, Dad!'

'Don't know about that,' Dad said. 'If Sam was my son I might take the risk.'

'PAU-AUL! You shouldn't joke about things like that.' Mum was glaring at him too now.

'Who says I'm joking?' Dad growled. The trouble is, Dad still blames Sam for most of Bella's problems at school, which if you ask me is a bit unfair.

'You know, believe it or not, Sam actually *liked* you when he first met you, Dad,' Bella said coldly.

'It's true,' I joined in. 'He told Bella you're not nearly as awful as *she's* always making out!'

I wasn't surprised by the jab in the ribs I got from Bella. Her sense of humour has been non-existent lately. So has Dad's, but at least he let out a snort that sounded vaguely like a laugh.

Bella put in her earphones and turned away to stare out of the window. It seems like she never stops scowling these days. I thought about what Mum had said when I'd complained to her about Bella being so mean and bad-tempered over the last few months. Mum said it wasn't uncommon for someone who was being bullied at school to take it out on their nearest and dearest. She said that now the bullying had stopped we just had to give Bella some time to revert to her normal self. Not that I was sure any more what Bella's normal self actually *is* …

'Let's play a game!' Grace said, giving my arm a tug. She didn't ask Bella, who would probably have ignored her in any case. Years ago, when Grace was a baby, Bella

8

and I had played loads of car games together on long journeys. Nowadays she prefers to retreat inside her own head whenever we're all in the car.

'OK then,' I agreed, even though I wouldn't have minded retreating too. But I knew that if I did I'd really disappoint Grace.

We played different games on and off for the next couple of hours while Bella listened to her music with her eyes closed. I could tell she wasn't asleep because she was nodding her head slightly in time with the beat. I tried to keep as much as possible to Grace's side of the car. At least she still likes cuddling up to me.

We were playing yet another round of 'Can you spot?' when Grace suddenly let out a whimper. I looked at her face and I knew at once what was wrong.

'Grace feels sick!' I shouted, which immediately set off Operation Sick Bowl.

'Can you get it for her, Libby? It's that empty ice-cream tub ... under Daddy's seat.'

'It's not here!'

'It must be!'

'Wait ... Nina, I think I might have put an ice-cream tub with the recycling when I cleaned out the car.'

'PAU-AUL!'

9

Bella had removed her earphones by this time. 'Libby gave her a book to read, Mum. That's probably what's done it.'

'LIBBY! You know she gets sick if she reads in the car!'

'She only had to look at the pictures! We're trying to spot a squirrel, aren't we, Grace?'

Grace mumbled something incomprehensible from behind the hand she'd clamped over her mouth.

Meanwhile, Mum was removing the lid from Dad's deluxe travel mug and peering inside saying, 'Sorry, Paul, but I'm not giving her my handbag ...'

Chapter Two

Dad had lowered his window to give Grace some fresh air, and by the time we reached the service station Bella's hair, much to my delight, was sticking out in all directions. (Mine probably was too but I didn't care.)

As we climbed out of the car Grace said she felt better.

'Better as in you're *not* going to hurl now?' Bella said sarcastically as she took out her hairbrush.

Grace looked puzzled. 'What's *hurl*?'

'It's just a cooler way to say being sick,' I explained.

Bella let out a dismissive snort. 'What do *you* know about being cool, Libby? *You're* certainly not!'

That comment got to me. I mean, I know I'm not cool, but I don't need *her* to tell me that.

At least I didn't have everyone at school texting horrible stuff about me, I felt like retaliating. But I couldn't say it – not knowing just how bad those texts had been.

Bella's problems at school had started six months earlier, though we hadn't known about it at the time. She'd had a big row with Sam's previous girlfriend, Andrea. That part was probably as much Bella's fault as Andrea's. But then Andrea started sending round nasty texts to all her mates, and also to Bella, accusing her of all sorts of things, including being unfaithful to Sam. The accusations and gossip became more and more vicious. Bella showed me some of the texts, but I knew there were also ones she deleted straight away because she said they were too disgusting to show anyone.

I didn't know what was happening when it all started. Bella didn't tell anyone at first, and at school the Year Sevens and Year Tens stayed pretty separate. But at home she was being really loud and mouthy, much more impatient than she'd ever been before, picking arguments with all of us, but especially with me. At the same time she started wanting to stay in all the time when she wasn't with Sam, and she never wanted me to go up and speak to anyone I knew from school if we were ever out and about together.

She was spending loads of time with Sam, who knew a bit about what was happening. He'd been sworn to secrecy by Bella, who threatened never to confide in him ever again if he told anyone. So he didn't tell, but instead he went round to Andrea's house to confront her about it and ended up getting punched by her older brother.

The cyberbullying (because I know now that's what it was) went on for a couple of months, until Mum saw a text one day and asked her about it. That was when Bella finally told our parents everything.

Mum and Dad were horrified and wanted to go to the school immediately, but they couldn't get an appointment to see the head teacher for several days. Apparently, when they did see him he wasn't that helpful, saying that the girls needed to sort it out themselves. Mum and Dad were furious with the school's attitude, and that's when they made up their minds to move Bella. But Dad was also furious with Sam for knowing about the texts and not telling him. He said that if Sam couldn't make the right decisions where Bella was concerned then he didn't want him seeing her any more. And when Bella told Dad defiantly that she was going to see Sam regardless, Dad grounded her for a fortnight.

Despite Bella being grounded, she and Sam were still texting all the time and facetiming each other loads. And as soon as she was free to go out again she carried on seeing Sam, though she was careful to do it behind Dad's back this time.

'Not seeing him just *hurts* too much,' she told me one evening, hugging her middle tightly as she spoke. 'But then I don't suppose you get that, do you?'

'Yes I do,' I said, enjoying the feeling of being confided in for once. 'It's like when Sarah left. I still really miss her.' Sarah had been my best friend since we'd started school together when we were five, but she moved away last year. We stayed in touch via email, but she quickly made another best friend at her new school. Not that I blamed her. I just wished that I'd been as quick to find someone else. Though now it didn't matter, I guess. I wondered if I would make a new best friend now that I was moving away too. Mum says it's better to have lots of different friends rather than one best one, because then if you fall out or they move away it doesn't matter so much. I'm sure she's right. In fact, I know from experience that she's right. So what is it that still makes me want to replace Sarah?

'It's not the same at all,' Bella had scoffed. 'But then you're such a baby. I should've known you wouldn't understand!'

If she hadn't had tears in her eyes as she spoke I might have argued back. Instead it struck me that she probably had a point. Yes, Sarah had been really important to me, but my family would always come first. Whereas if Bella had to choose between Sam and us at that moment ... well, let's just say I wasn't so confident who would win.

By the start of July, Mum and Dad were having problems trying to find a new school for Bella. It didn't help that she was sitting GCSEs next year and her predicted grades weren't very good. That's when Aunt Thecla stepped in and suggested we move to live near her and let her pay the fees for all three of us to go to the independent school she had attended herself. It was called St Clara's and Aunt Thecla knew the headmistress there. Apparently they had places for all three of us for the coming school year.

'Over my dead body!' was Dad's first response. 'There's no way on earth I'm going back to live in that village.'

'Paul, let's just go and have a look,' Mum had said in her most persuasive voice. When Dad still refused to budge she'd said, 'Think about it, Paul. It's girls only. That means no boys to distract Bella. Or Libby and Grace when the time comes.'

That had sparked Dad's interest a bit. Then Mum added, 'We'd also be putting some distance between Bella and Sam.'

The following day Dad had called us all together. 'Your mother and I have been thinking … we're going to look at St Clara's, and if we like it we'll move. But we're going to rent out our house here and rent a place in the village close to the school. A year will be long enough to get Bella through her GCSEs. Then if we decide not to stay we can just move back.'

I was about to protest that Bella wasn't the only one in our family, and that just because I didn't have any problems at school *yet* it didn't mean I wouldn't have if I had to keep moving around. But Mum gave me a look that promised she had no intention of moving back even if she wasn't about to contradict Dad at this point. So I let it rest.

Everything happened super-fast after that. We went to visit St Clara's, where we met with the headmistress, Mrs McLusky, and we were all offered places to start after the summer holiday. Mum managed to get herself some part-time work at the dental practice in the village, and Dad has his own business as a web designer working mainly from home, so that was fine.

I have to say that I'd half expected Bella to stage a sit-in at the last minute and totally refuse to leave our house. But after meeting Sam for lunch the day before we left she'd seemed surprisingly calm about things. Which just goes to show that Sam is actually a pretty good influence on her, rather than a disruptive one as Mum and Dad seem to think.

Chapter Three

Unfortunately, now that we were leaving, Mum and Dad would never get to see that side of Sam – the side that's really kind and protective.

I thought back to when I'd first seen it myself. It was soon after our elderly cat Trixie died. I'd made a little wooden cross to mark the spot where Dad had buried her at the far end of our garden. As I sat by her grave one afternoon telling her how much I missed her I heard someone approaching and assumed it was Mum or Bella.

'Hi, Libby,' said an unexpected male voice, and I felt myself squirm as I realised Sam must have heard me talking to our dead cat.

'Oh …' I stood up abruptly. 'Hi …'

Bella had only been going out with him for a few weeks and it was the third or fourth time he'd been round to our house. It was before he'd dropped out of his A levels so the only concrete thing Dad had against him at that point was that he'd been suspended from school for a week at the end of Year Eleven for calling our headmaster 'useless and spineless'. (Dad said that even though it was true, it showed gross stupidity and immaturity to actually call the man that to his face.) There was also the fact that Sam was in the sixth form, whereas Bella was only in Year Ten. Dad has always had a big problem with that, even though the actual age difference is only fourteen months.

'Hi,' he said. 'Bella said to come and give you this out here so your mum doesn't see.' As he spoke he handed me a framed photograph of Trixie. She was lying in her favourite spot in the sun on top of Bella's bed. I immediately felt tears in my eyes. It was exactly how I wanted to remember her.

'I gave a copy to Bella too,' Sam said. 'I took it the last time I came round.' He looked a bit self-conscious as he added, 'Listen, you can't tell your parents I actually took those photos or they'll know I was in Bella's room, OK?'

I nodded. I really wished I *could* tell Mum and Dad about the photos so they would see for themselves how kind Sam could be. I knew I couldn't though. Bella had been at home on her own that day and Sam wasn't meant to have been here at all, let alone in Bella's bedroom. I knew that Dad would go ballistic if he found out.

'It's lovely, Sam. Thank you,' I murmured. I have to say I was pretty touched that he'd thought of me as well as Bella.

'That's OK. I know how bad it is to lose a pet you've grown up with.'

'Has it happened to you?' I asked softly.

He nodded. 'I had a cat called Mabel. I got her when she was a kitten. Last year my mum gave her away without even asking me, just because she kept scratching the new carpet.'

'Oh, Sam … that's terrible.' And that's when I decided I liked him.

A few months later Dad did catch Bella and Sam alone in our house – though thankfully not in her bedroom. It happened one afternoon when Dad came home early from a meeting in town. It was Sam's half-day and Bella had skipped school so she could hang out with him at our place. Dad was totally furious, especially with Sam. He accused him of being irresponsible and disobedient, and a few other things on top, before shoving him out the door. Later he went round to complain to Sam's mother, who turned out to be less than helpful. (Apparently she said, 'He's not a child. He's seventeen – the same age I was when I had him. You have a problem with him seeing your girl, then speak to *him* about it! And maybe you should speak to *her* at the same time!')

'Well, she's got a point,' Mum said when Dad reported back to her. 'He's *not* a child. Neither is Bella for that matter.'

'They're both still young enough to accept *some* parental guidance,' Dad snapped, 'though I can see that for Sam it's not exactly abundant!'

'Poor kid,' Mum murmured.

For a moment Dad looked like he might be thinking the same, but then his face hardened. 'We have to think about Bella and what's best for her,' he reminded Mum firmly. 'The sooner she stops seeing him the better.'

I almost spoke up and told them that in my opinion splitting them up wasn't actually in Bella's best interests at all. But as usual I kept quiet. I might be good at noticing things that other people don't, but unfortunately I'm not so good at having the confidence to actually share those things with people – especially when I don't think they'll agree with me.

* * *

'So, girls? How are we feeling?' Dad asked Bella and me. We were inside the service station waiting for Mum and Grace, who were taking ages in the Ladies. I could tell Dad really wanted to hear that we were feeling OK about moving to live in the country.

'I've never felt so miserable,' Bella told him flatly.

I waited for Dad to check if I felt the same way, but he didn't. I don't think it was because he didn't care about my feelings. I just think he sometimes finds Bella's feelings so much to handle that he hasn't got room to ask me about mine as well.

He looked worried as he launched straight into trying to coax my sister out of her bad mood, the way he'd always done so easily when she was younger.

'Sweetheart … cheer up … you know this is your chance for a fresh start. And you have to do your GCSEs somewhere. You liked the school when we looked around, didn't you?'

'It's not the school that's the problem,' Bella said sharply. 'It's everything else. I mean, we don't know anybody and we've absolutely no friends there.'

'No enemies either,' I pointed out.

'*Yet*,' she emphasised with feeling.

22

'Come on, Bella ...' Dad persisted. 'We'll all support each other, and I bet you'll make friends in no time.'

'And just *think*,' Bella continued doggedly. 'Instead of seeing Aunt Thecla twice a year, she'll be living down the road from us. Can you imagine how it'll be having her constantly commenting on Grace's table manners and trying to estimate what size feet Libby will end up with and going on and on at me to eat more vegetables ...'

'Oh Bella, I'm sure it won't be that bad.'

'Yes it will. And she'll be coming to every sports day and school concert, telling everyone she's our aunt and wanting to know the reason why if we don't get starring roles. I mean how gruesome is that?'

Dad swallowed and I could tell he was remembering the same incident we all were – the time when Aunt Thecla came to watch my school Nativity play one Christmas and marched up to the teacher at the end, demanding – in her loud, posh voice – to know why I was a shepherd for the second year running. Dad banned her from coming to my school plays after that, even though she did apologise and explain that she found it hard to watch me being 'overlooked' (as she saw it) when Bella had been Mary in Reception, Angel Gabriel in Year One and the only king with a speaking part in Year Two. And

23

I remember that in among all the embarrassment I felt quite surprised and pleased that she would stand up for me like that.

'At least she won't have to stay with us for the whole week at Christmas any more,' I pointed out to Bella. 'Or even overnight.'

'Thank God,' Bella said with a snort.

'For small mercies,' I added with a grin, because that's one of our aunt's favourite sayings.

Dad sighed. 'You know, despite how difficult your aunt can be at times, you girls are very important to her. Family is everything as far as she's concerned – and we're all she's got. I want you to try and remember that.'

That was rich coming from him, I thought.

'What about *our* family?' Bella demanded. 'Mum and you and the three of *us*. Isn't that important too?'

'Of course it is.'

'Because in case you haven't noticed, the only time you and Mum argue really badly is when Aunt Thecla comes to stay. I just hope moving here doesn't put too much strain on your marriage, that's all.'

Dad's mouth fell open, like it had been doing a lot lately after Bella had spoken. And this time he found himself with absolutely nothing to say in response.

Chapter Four

As my sisters and I walked back to our car ahead of Mum and Dad, Bella seemed to have whipped herself up into a new state of bad temper. 'Oh look, guys, you can tick off "squirrel"!' she declared in a mocking tone.

'Where?' Grace asked excitedly.

'If it's dead it doesn't count,' I said, having already spotted the remains of a small furry creature on the grey tarmac close to the exit road. 'Don't worry, Gracie. We'll see plenty of live squirrels in the countryside … rabbits too, I expect.'

Grace was frowning. 'How will we make sure we don't run them over?'

'Oh, I wouldn't worry about it,' Bella said. 'Dad says when you live in the country you've got to expect a bit of roadkill.'

'BELLA!' I snapped crossly.

'What's roadkill?' Grace wanted to know.

'It's what you call an animal that's been run over. If it's fresh and not too badly mangled, you can take it home and eat it,' Bella informed her.

Grace's mouth had fallen open. 'You're lying!'

'I'm not. You can't afford to be squeamish about these things in the countryside, Gracie. Did you know when Dad was a boy his father used to take him out *shooting* rabbits?'

'BELLA!' I snarled. 'He did *not*!'

'Yes he did. Aunt Thecla told me. They used to make rabbit pies.'

Grace's face had gone pale and she looked like she might be starting to feel sick again.

'Stop being so mean,' I said, because I knew exactly what Bella was doing. She was trying to make Grace feel as bad about moving as she did.

Bella has done the same thing to me plenty of times in the past. It's as if she can't stand me not being equally upset about anything that's upsetting her. The most notable time was when Grace was born. That was when I was six and Bella was nine. We were really close in those days. At primary school Bella was confident and popular, whereas I was shy and tended to stay in the background.

She would always stand up for me and help me out if anything went wrong, and I used to follow her around – both at home and at school – like a faithful puppy. But when Grace was born I remember being excited and wanting to help Mum with our new baby, whereas Bella was more worried about the baby taking up all of Mum's time.

After a couple of days of failing to get me to see that our new baby sister was going to be a big problem for both of us, she told me she felt especially sorry for me because I was now a 'middle child'. According to Bella, it was a well-known fact that parents didn't love middle children as much as the oldest and youngest ones. I got really upset, until Mum found out about it and reassured me that she loved me just as much as she always had. I suppose, looking back, Bella just needed *me* to feel as jealous and insecure as she clearly felt at the time.

We stayed close until she hit her teens, when I guess she just became less interested in having me trailing around as her loyal sidekick and Number One Fan. She seemed to stop confiding in me, and whenever I tried to get her to open up the way she used to she'd snap that I was 'too young' or 'too immature' to understand whatever it was she was worrying about. Gradually more and more distance grew between us. She became a lot more self-conscious and the list of things she found embarrassing was endless. And the worst thing was that I seemed to be on this list!

Ever since I'd started Year Seven she'd hassled me on and off about my appearance, making me worry about things I'd been totally relaxed about before – my hairstyle, my shoes, even the coat I wore. She'd warned me that I was 'prone to looking dorky' and that I needed to 'keep on top of it' if I didn't want to end up in the dorky group. She said it didn't help that I was always sucking up to my teachers, and whenever I put lots of effort into my homework or got especially high marks for some piece of work, all I heard was, 'You're such a swot!' or 'It's just not cool!'.

Strangely it was Aunt Thecla who stood up for me about that. She happened to be staying with us one time when Bella was having a go at me for getting top marks in a history test. Suddenly Aunt Thecla declared, 'My dear Bella, I do feel sorry for you! It's always *so* horrible to feel jealous. Believe me, I've been there myself many times – so exhausting and unpleasant!'

'Unpleasant for *me*, you mean!' I said.

She shook her head. 'One thing you ought to know by now, Elisabeth, is that I always say exactly what I mean.'

I still couldn't accept that Bella could ever be envious of me. After all, she was the cool older sister while I was the dorky younger one. 'You're not jealous, are you, Bella?' I said with a dismissive laugh.

'Of course not!' But she'd looked sulky and slightly pink in the face all the same.

Dad's phone rang when we were back on the motorway, so Mum answered it for him. We could tell by the way Mum spoke that it was Aunt Thecla. Mum always sounds a bit impatient whenever she has to speak to her, chiefly because Aunt Thecla always asks too many questions. 'Yes, Thecla. Don't worry, Thecla. We'll phone you when we arrive at the cottage.' She came off the phone saying, 'Honestly, it's like she *wants* this cottage to turn out to be awful, just so she's proved right.'

Aunt Thecla had wanted to find us a house to rent in the village, and she'd been horrified when Mum had looked online and found a quaint little country cottage that wasn't actually in the village itself. Aunt Thecla had done her best to put Mum off by telling her that the lady who was renting it out also lived in the village and she'd met her a couple of times and hadn't liked her. But Mum said Mrs Fuller had seemed perfectly nice when they'd spoken on the phone. 'She seemed very relaxed about everything,' Mum told us. 'The complete opposite of Thecla, so I can see why they wouldn't get along.'

'Well, I agree with Aunt Thecla for once,' Bella piped up now. 'At least if we were renting a house in the village then we could *walk* to school and *walk* to the shops and stuff.'

'There isn't much "stuff" to walk to, Bella, not even in the village,' Dad warned her gently. 'You'll need to go to Castle Westbury, which is our nearest town, if you want proper shops.'

'And if we'd rented in the village like Thecla sugges-ted, then *she* could just *walk* to see us whenever she liked,' Mum put in, not so gently.

'Well, *I* think our cottage sounds really sweet,' I said before Mum and Bella could start arguing about it. I'd loved the photos of the cottage. According to the online advert it was situated in a small hamlet just a few miles from the village itself. There were three cottages in total, set back from the road in a little row, with gardens that backed on to a field with horses in it. Grace was really excited when she heard about the horses, and even I had started thinking about the possibility of riding lessons.

30

I was soon lost in a daydream about my perfect pony, thinking up names for it and closing my eyes to better imagine how it looked. I must have dozed off because soon I was dreaming about a pony disappearing into the distance with Bella on its back. And in the dream I couldn't work out if Bella was riding away from us on purpose or because she didn't have any control over her pony.

When I woke up I realised I must have been asleep for ages because we'd left the motorway and Mum was driving instead of Dad. We were crawling along behind a tractor on a windy country road and through the rear window I could see a long queue of cars behind us.

'You have to be *brave* about overtaking in the country, Mum,' Bella was saying impatiently. 'Otherwise you're going to get stuck behind tractors all the time.'

'Be quiet, Bella,' Mum snapped.

But of course Bella didn't. 'Hey, did you know Aunt Thecla's overtaking record is two tractors with *four* cars in between?'

'Now that's what we country folk call a tractor sandwich,' Dad joked.

We all laughed except Mum, who said, 'Really? Well, that's what *I* call driving like a maniac!'

Chapter Five

I guess it's fair to say that Aunt Thecla is the kind of person who tends to have a considerable impact on those around her.

Dad always describes her as 'a very formidable lady', and it's true that she does tend to make a lasting impression wherever she goes. She's tall with broad shoulders and she has what Mum calls a 'big-boned' sort of build. She also has thick dark hair with white streaks through it, and Bella once joked that she looks like Cruella de Vil. She has these dark grey, almost-black eyes that turn really glinty and sharp if she doesn't approve of something or someone. They've never got too glinty or sharp with me thank goodness, but I've seen it happen with other people, and she's probably the only person alive who can make Dad squirm.

Bella says I'm her favourite and I think maybe she's right. I'm not really sure why she gets on better with me than with my sisters, but I think it might be because they don't have a lot to do with her when she visits, whereas I find all her stories about the past quite interesting and I don't mind sitting and listening. I even ask questions, which Bella gets cross about because she says it just encourages her to talk even more.

Then there's the fact that Aunt Thecla freely admits to not liking very many people. 'I can't help it if I'm not a people person,' she'll say with no embarrassment at all. And she'll declare, 'The trouble with most friends is that they are far too demanding of one's time. That's why I like to keep mine to a minimum. Quality not quantity – that's the important thing.'

Dad says he can't imagine too many people wanting to be Aunt Thecla's friend in any case. 'It's all very well being rude and critical to your family, but you can't get away with that with friends.'

Our aunt was fifty last year, and even though that's actually only a couple of years older than Dad, she's always seemed like his much older sister. She's never married or had any children, but according to Dad she was engaged once when she was very young. I've tried to ask her about it a couple of times, but that's the one thing she never seems to want to talk about.

A long time ago she worked as a history teacher at St Clara's, but at some point she gave that up to look after our grandfather. I think she looked after him for quite a long time, until he died several years ago. Then she sold the family home (for an absolute fortune, according to Mum) and downsized to her current house in the village. I think she might have tried to give Dad some of the money from the house, but he refused because he hated his father so much. I remember hearing Mum and Dad arguing about it one time.

I don't know much about my grandfather. Dad hadn't spoken to him in years, and none of us – not even Mum – ever actually met him. It was after he died that we started to see more of Aunt Thecla. She always visited us rather than the other way round, and the first time we'd been to her house and seen the village where Dad grew up was when we came to look at our new school.

Every time our aunt came to stay with us Mum would start off being very polite to her, but she could never keep it up for more than the first twenty-four hours, after which time they'd begin snapping at each other because Aunt Thecla would start dishing out advice, which Dad can't bear. He always seemed to have lots of work on whenever she came, and he'd disappear as much as he could, which then set Mum off snapping at him.

The atmosphere got particularly tense during Aunt Thecla's visit to us last August. The year before she'd adopted a West Highland Terrier called Hughie, who was very boisterous, very yappy and very possessive of her. He was also quite smelly and had bits of dried poo stuck to the dirty white fur around his bottom, which our aunt never seemed to notice. Needless to say, none of my family were exactly wild about him, even though Dad, Bella, Grace and I really like most dogs (whereas Mum is more of a cat person).

Anyway, last summer our aunt had offered to pay for our elderly cat Trixie to stay in a cattery so that she could bring Hughie with her, and Mum had just about had a fit. She was pretty soppy about Trixie, who she'd had since she was a tiny kitten, a couple of years before Bella was born. 'So poor Hughie can't possibly stay in kennels, but it doesn't matter if poor arthritic old Trixie pines away in the cattery!' she exclaimed when Dad told her.

'Don't worry, Nina. I told her it was out of the question,' he reassured her. 'I said that Trixie can't do without her home comforts now that she's such an old lady.'

'Good! And what did she say to that?'

'She asked me how long cats live for,' Dad said with a grin, which he quickly killed when he saw Mum's face. He can sometimes see the funny side when it comes to our aunt. To be fair, so can Mum. I guess the trouble is that they never seem to see it at the same time.

Anyway, Aunt Thecla arrived the following week, and after she'd been chatting and drinking tea for half an hour she asked where Trixie was.

'Oh, she'll be outside somewhere, I expect,' Mum said.

'Good … now, Nina, there's something I have to confess … I know I agreed not to bring Hughie, but he was so distressed when I tried to drop him at the kennels this morning that I just couldn't do it … and, after all, if the cat is out most of the time she's hardly going to even notice he's here, is she?'

Mum's mouth literally fell open as Aunt Thecla left the kitchen to go and fetch Hughie from the car.

So Hughie ended up sleeping on our aunt's bed for the whole week, and poor Trixie nearly had a fit every time she caught sight of him or heard him barking. She hardly came inside for the entire week, and even after Aunt Thecla left it took Trixie a whole day to come in from the bottom of the garden. Once she did she started weeing in the house on a daily basis, which we all thought was her marking her territory, until Mum eventually took her to the vet, who discovered a big inoperable lump in her tummy. So a week later Mum was in floods of tears as she took her to be put down.

Mum said that she knew it was irrational to blame Aunt Thecla for Trixie's death – and even more irrational to blame Hughie – but she couldn't help holding them responsible for making the end of Trixie's life so miserable.

'The trouble with Thecla is that she only thinks about herself,' Mum said. 'Which is what comes of living on your own for so long, I suppose.'

But Dad shook his head. 'She was born like it. Totally self-absorbed from day one, that's her.'

Mum avoided talking to Aunt Thecla on the phone over the next few months and said there was no way Hughie was ever coming to our house again. In fact, it sounded like our aunt wouldn't be welcome for the foreseeable future either.

It was only when Aunt Thecla phoned in tears six months later to tell us that Hughie had been run over by a car that Mum forgave her and started speaking to her again.

Chapter Six

'Not far now, girls,' Mum said, slowing down as a guy on a motorbike overtook us.

'Is that Sam?' Grace asked.

'Shut up, Grace,' Bella hissed.

'Sam doesn't have a motorbike,' I said with a yawn.

'Yes he does!' Grace insisted. 'Bella's ridden on it, haven't you, Bella?'

I turned to look at my older sister, who was now glaring at Grace.

'Excuse me?' Dad turned round in his seat to look at both of them.

'Paul, calm down!' Mum said impatiently. 'It was a short ride and she was wearing a helmet and all the proper protective clothing –'

'Wait … you mean it's true? And you *knew*?'

'Grace saw them from the window. I didn't tell you because I knew you'd be upset, and Bella promised that would be the end of it.'

'It shouldn't have happened at all! So when did he get a licence? That's assuming he actually *has* a licence ... and does he actually own this motorbike?'

'His uncle lent him the money for it when he turned seventeen,' Bella snapped. 'And of course he's got a licence!'

Dad snorted disapprovingly. 'Bella, have you any idea how vulnerable a motorcyclist is if they're involved in a collision?'

'I should have,' Bella muttered under her breath. 'You've told us often enough.'

'Paul, that car behind is trying to overtake us,' Mum suddenly said sharply. 'And I can't even see round this tractor!'

She blasted the horn really loudly as the car behind started to overtake both us and the tractor.

'Nina – take it easy,' Dad said, reaching up to clutch the handle above his door. Mum gets really cross when he does that but luckily she didn't see.

'Don't tell *me* to take it easy, Paul!' Mum snapped. 'It's these country drivers that are the problem! Look, here's another one trying to overtake me – no patience, any of them! So much for life running at a slower pace in the country!'

Dad didn't comment but I noticed he kept hold of his grab handle.

'Look – there's a sign for the school,' Bella suddenly said. 'We must be really close now.'

I saw the sign too: *St Clara's School for Girls aged 4 to 18*. And I think that's when my stomach did a flip and our move to the countryside started to feel … well … just a lot more *real*.

As we turned the last bend in the road and saw the trio of cottages Mum exclaimed in relief, 'Here we are!'

My sisters and I cheered.

'Well, at least she's not here yet,' Dad grunted.

Aunt Thecla had phoned for another update fifteen minutes earlier, and when she found out how close we were she said she would set off straight away and meet us at the cottage. Mum tried to dissuade her but she refused to take no for an answer. She had bought some shopping for us, plus she wanted to inspect the inside of the cottage herself. No doubt if she didn't think it was clean enough she'd ignore Mum's protests and start vacuuming carpets and washing windows around us while we were unpacking our stuff, whether it was convenient or not.

Mum parked up on the grass verge in front of the cottages – ours was the first one of the three – and we all piled out. 'Mrs Fuller said she'd leave the key under the flower pot,' Mum said.

While Dad and Bella headed for the front door Grace and I raced round to the rear of the house, hoping to see the horses. The back garden was so overgrown that we couldn't easily cross it, so we stayed at the top by the house and looked down to the field at the bottom. A couple of horses were grazing at the far side and we could hear a dog barking somewhere nearby.

The sound of a car, together with a yell from Bella caught our attention. 'AUNT THECLA'S HERE!'

When we returned to the front of the house our aunt was already out of her car and greeting Mum with a peck on her cheek, while Dad stood back, presumably to stop her from kissing *him*. Mum always says that Dad turns into a bit of a teenager when Aunt Thecla is around, and he certainly looked like one with the stubborn face he was pulling right now.

'My, haven't you all grown,' she exclaimed.

'Yeah, well ... kids tend to do that so long as they're getting fed,' Dad grunted.

Bella sniggered and Mum shot him a quick glare.

If I was Aunt Thecla I certainly wouldn't have tried to kiss Bella at that moment, but of course Aunt Thecla isn't known for her super-awareness of other people's feelings. Bella stood rigid as she flung her arms around her, and they ended up in a really awkward collision rather than an embrace.

I would have laughed, but I knew it was my turn next.

As our aunt approached me she gushed, 'Look how much *you've* grown, Elisabeth ... goodness ... you're quite the young lady now ...' She was staring at my chest as she spoke and I felt myself blushing. My boobs aren't that big but they're definitely there now, whereas they probably weren't the last time she saw me. 'Do you know, I can see you looking more and more like your grandmother,' she informed me. 'I believe she was quite a big girl too at your age.'

Bella gave a little snort while I flushed scarlet. Aunt Thecla is always coming out with things that make me cringe, even when she's trying to be complimentary. (Mum says it's because she verbalises everything she's thinking without stopping to filter it first. Dad says she's just plain tactless.)

I was named Elisabeth after my grandmother, who died when Dad and Aunt Thecla were teenagers. I know they both loved her very much, and I know my aunt thinks she's paying me a compliment when she says I'm like her. The trouble is I've seen photos of my grandmother, who was a plain plumpish lady with wiry reddish hair and freckles, who I'm not that wild about being the spitting image of. Bella thinks it's hilarious of course.

'And, Grace, *your* face has changed again,' our aunt was observing now. 'I really think I'm starting to see your grandfather's chin.'

Finally Dad couldn't keep quiet. '*I* think you need to get your eyes checked, Thecla,' he said in an irritated voice. 'Grace looks nothing like our father.'

Mentioning our grandfather in front of Dad is never a good idea. Like I said before, Dad broke off all contact with him before any of us were even born. He's always refused to tell us why they fell out, except to say his father was an 'utterly ruthless and selfish man' and that he doesn't want to talk about him.

Dad went back to battling with the front door of the cottage, which he still hadn't managed to open.

43

'I expect the wood's swollen with all the rain we've had,' our aunt said in her usual know-it-all voice. 'If I were you I'd give it a good kick.'

Dad scowled because he hates Aunt Thecla telling him what to do. He kicked the bottom of the door and it made a sort of squeaky scraping noise. Then he kicked harder and it opened. At the same time we could hear a dog in one of the other cottages barking loudly.

'Girls, you need to watch where you're walking,' our aunt warned us in a loud voice as she pointed to a pile of dog poo in the grass. 'The dogs next door don't care whose garden they do their business in, and I'm afraid not everyone around here is as committed as they should be to "poop and scoop".'

'Come on then, girls,' Mum said swiftly. 'Let's take a look at our new home.' I suspected she was as anxious as we were to get our aunt inside before she totally offended our new neighbours.

I was the last person to enter, aside from Aunt Thecla, who was busy inspecting the garden for more dog poo. I found Bella, Dad and Mum standing absolutely still in the middle of the living room.

'Oh ...' I murmured as I took in the faded threadbare

carpet and the ancient green velvet-covered settee. 'It looked a lot smarter in the pictures, didn't it?'

Mum's face couldn't hide her disappointment, and nor could Dad's. Bella was looking frankly horrified.

Grace had gone to check out the upstairs, and now she came hurtling back down the steep staircase that went straight up from the room we were in. 'Careful!' Mum called, but even as she spoke the ancient-looking wooden handrail shifted under the weight of Grace's hand. She screamed as the top end gave way and she only just managed to let go in time as the whole thing swung outwards.

Dad rushed over to her, and after he'd checked she was OK he looked at the broken handrail with disgust. 'That should have been fixed before we got here.'

Suddenly Aunt Thecla arrived in the doorway. 'I suppose I'd better take off my shoes before I come in –' she began, breaking off abruptly as she took in her surroundings. She crinkled her nose as her gaze settled on the grubby-looking carpet. 'Or perhaps I'd better keep them on.'

Chapter Seven

'How many sleeps till we start our new school?' Grace asked as the three of us got ready for bed in Mum and Dad's room that night. Grace had a tiny single room next to theirs, while Bella and I shared the musty-smelling twin-bedded room across the landing.

'Oh, Grace, it's not for ages yet –' I began.

'Three weeks,' Mum said as she came in to help her find her pyjamas. 'Are you excited about it, Gracie?'

There was a brief silence, then, 'Mummy, if I don't like my new school can I go back to my old one?'

'No,' Bella snapped, before Mum had time to answer. When Mum glared at her, Bella said stroppily, 'Well, it's true, isn't it? You're *not* going to let us go back.'

Mum was silent. I guess there wasn't much she could say to that since essentially Bella was right. Bella's bad mood wasn't making this easier for any of us though.

46

'Grace, I expect you *will* like it because you're going to be at the same school as Bella and me,' I said, trying to make her feel better.

Grace said nothing but she looked like she was thinking about something worrying. She stayed quiet for a little while longer then said, 'Remember that painting of the dead fox that Aunt Thecla gave Daddy for his birthday? The one she painted herself and Daddy said was more real-looking than he'd expected?'

'Yes,' Mum and I said together, wondering where this was going.

'Was *that* road killed, do you think?'

'Oh … well …' Mum and I looked at each other, both of us floundering.

'Maybe … but then at least it wasn't ripped apart by hounds,' Bella said sarcastically before she disappeared into the only bathroom and slammed the door behind her.

Once Bella and I were alone in our bedroom she said, 'Hey, do you know the only *good* thing about renting this place?'

'What?' I asked suspiciously, because I was struggling to find anything good about it right now. Our room was small and dark with a low ceiling and it smelt really odd.

According to Bella the smell was probably a mix of damp, mould and dust, and she said it was a good job neither of us has asthma.

'At least Aunt Thecla's hideous paintings have to stay in storage!' she declared.

I smiled. 'That's true! But it's going to be tricky now we're living so close to her, isn't it? I mean, we can't just put up her paintings for the week she's staying with us.'

'Sam thinks it's hilarious how Mum and Dad do that,' Bella said.

Suddenly Mum appeared in our doorway, looking anxious.

'Have you two brushed your teeth yet?'

'Yes, Mum!' Bella answered with a roll of her eyes. '*And* flossed.'

'Why? What's wrong, Mum?' I asked when she didn't look nearly as satisfied as she normally would.

Then Dad appeared behind her, holding a large bottle of mineral water. 'It definitely comes from a tank in the loft, Nina … full of animal droppings and dead bats, most likely …'

'What are you talking about?' Bella demanded.

'The water in the bathroom. Make sure you don't drink any of it. In fact, I wouldn't even use it to brush your –'

48

He broke off as Bella let out a fake retching sound and I murmured, 'I think I'm going to be sick.'

After Mum and Dad had gone, Bella hissed angrily, 'I hate it here! I wish –' She broke off abruptly as her phone buzzed. We'd had an intermittent signal since we'd arrived – more absent than present – and now it seemed the outside world was finally getting through.

'Is it Sam?' I prompted as I watched Bella read the text.

'Shush!' She swiftly turned on to her side away from me and started texting back, shutting me out again, just like she usually did.

The first couple of days in our rented cottage turned out to be anything but idyllic. Yes, it looked like a quaint little country cottage on the outside and, yes, it was right next to a field with horses in it and, yes, there was a riding school just along the road and a farm nearby which sold freshly laid eggs. But actual day-to-day life soon turned out to be a sort of endurance test.

First, the ancient boiler kept switching off, leaving us with no hot water, and now that we'd got the front door open it wouldn't close properly. On day two, Dad lost his temper and kicked the door shut with so much force that one of the rusty hinges broke off, so we had to get a joiner in to repair it and plane some wood off the bottom of the door at the same time. The joiner looked at the staircase handrail and said it could do with replacing, but Mrs Fuller refused to have that done, claiming there had been nothing wrong with the handrail until we'd set foot in her house. Instead she sent her husband round to fix it back on so that it looked OK again, though Mum and Dad kept reminding us to be careful as we weren't sure how secure it was.

On day three it rained and we discovered several holes in the roof, one of which was directly above my bed. Mum said that must be why our bedroom smelt so badly of damp. The only positive thing was that Dad climbed up into the loft that day and found that the water storage tank had a cover on it. Which was just as well because at night we'd definitely heard some weird scratching noises overhead.

Sam was texting Bella several times a day, though because of the bad signal she often wouldn't get any of his messages until we left the cottage. I guessed Sam must be missing Bella a lot, though funnily enough *she* didn't seem to be missing *him* as much as I'd anticipated. I'd expected her to shut herself away and refuse to show any interest at all in our new surroundings. In fact, she seemed keen to go out and about exploring, though she never wanted any of us to go with her.

On day four Grace said she'd seen a gerbil in the garden and she got all excited because she thought it must be someone's pet that had escaped from its cage. She spent all afternoon outside on the patio trying to lure it into an empty shoebox with little squares of peanut butter on toast, because according to Grace that's what gerbils like to eat.

We didn't take much notice until lunchtime the following day when we were all sitting at the table by the window eating sandwiches.

'Oh look, there are two of them now!' Grace suddenly said enthusiastically.

Mum looked out at the patio and screamed.

Two large rats were feeding on the scraps Grace had put down. 'Right, that's it, Paul! We're not staying here!' Mum blurted.

'They're only rats, Nina.'

Mum immediately started listing off all the horrible diseases rats can pass on to humans: 'Typhoid fever, rat-bite fever, tapeworm, salmonellosis, leptospirosis, toxoplasmosis, bubonic plague –'

'OK, OK, don't panic. I'll put down some poison,' Dad said impatiently.

Grace burst into tears. 'You can't poison them, Daddy! It's cruel!' She became completely hysterical when he offered to set some traps to kill them with instead.

'Hey, what if those scratchy noises in the loft are rats?' Bella said. 'What if they're *inside* the house as well?'

That afternoon Mum and Dad went to see our land-lady, Mrs Fuller. Mum was usually perfectly happy to leave us in the house alone for short periods, but today she invited Aunt Thecla over to stay with us while they were gone.

'Are you sure that's necessary, Nina?' Dad said, trying to dissuade her. 'The countryside is much safer than the town, you know.'

But Mum wouldn't be swayed and said that the countryside in general might be safer, but this particular cottage was a whole different matter.

Of course, as soon as Aunt Thecla arrived she was bursting with 'I told you so'. Having seen and smelt our bedroom she offered to put up Bella and me in her spare room straight away. She didn't offer for Grace to come with us. I think even she knows that Grace is too much of a mummy's girl to agree. Besides, Grace's bedroom wasn't nearly as toxic as ours.

I'd expected Bella to kick up a fuss about moving in with Aunt Thecla, even for a short while, but to my surprise she readily agreed. 'That would be brilliant, Aunt Thecla!' she said, rewarding her with an unusually warm smile.

So that evening Bella and I left Rat Cottage (as Bella had christened it) and moved in with Aunt Thecla, while Mum and Dad began their search for alternative accommodation in the village.

Chapter Eight

A few days later I woke up in the room I was sharing with Bella at Aunt Thecla's house, feeling gloomy. The large depressing painting of withered bluebells in a cracked black vase on the wall above the bed didn't help either. I really missed my old bedroom. It wasn't very big but it had always given me somewhere to wind down. Mum had let me choose the colour scheme myself, and my window had overlooked the back garden.

I realised I was feeling a lot like I'd felt just after Sarah left – kind of bored with everything, as if I couldn't be bothered leaving the house or making much of an effort to do anything. And I was worrying about school. It was still the summer holidays at the moment, but in a few weeks I would have to make a huge effort to be sociable whether I felt like it or not. There was no going back home to my old house and my old school, which, even if

I'd never exactly loved it, was at least reassuringly familiar.

I suppose I'd been hoping this move would bring Bella and me a bit closer, since neither of us had any friends here. I was hoping we'd have to rely on each other for company, at least until school started, but instead Bella seemed to be avoiding everyone. Since we'd moved in with our aunt she kept saying that she wanted to go out on her own to explore the village, and she was full of excuses about why I couldn't go with her. Whenever she came home she always seemed pretty chirpy for someone who'd spent the whole day hanging out alone. I did try to press her for more information about where she'd been, certain she wasn't telling the whole truth, but she always got snarky and told me to mind my own business.

Aunt Thecla wasn't much company either. She spent most of the day up in her attic studio, where she told us she was working on a portrait of her beloved Hughie. I asked if I could see it but she refused to let me even enter her art room. It was off limits to everyone, with no exceptions, she said, although she did promise to show me the painting as soon as she'd finished it to her satisfaction.

'To *her* satisfaction being the key point,' Bella said sarcastically when I told her.

I giggled because it was true that our aunt's whole house was full of awful paintings that had clearly also been completed to her own satisfaction.

So any worries I'd had of having to spend hours on my own being polite to Aunt Thecla turned out to be quite unfounded, since she was far too obsessed with depicting Hughie to bother too much about me. She would appear in the living room from time to time to criticise my TV watching, but I usually ignored her since there was nothing else to do to pass the time.

Today I got up to find Bella already downstairs and fully dressed. She was sitting on top of the kitchen unit by the fridge, reading something on her phone as she munched on a banana. Aunt Thecla wasn't there or she'd have been nagging her to sit down and eat a proper breakfast at the table.

'I wonder if Aunt Thecla will ever get another dog,' I said, more to get her attention than anything else.

'The house still stinks of Hughie,' Bella complained, still not looking up from her phone. 'Hey, listen to this ... Thecla is the name of a saint.' She started reading from her phone screen. 'Thecla was a saint in the early Christian Church who was saved from burning at the stake by a miraculous storm, sentenced to be eaten by wild beasts, then saved again by a series of miracles.' She started to laugh.

'Well, I've never heard of her,' I said with a grin as I put some bread in the toaster.

'There are probably loads of saints you've never heard of,' Bella said. 'Hey, did you know Mum told me she might go to church with Aunt Thecla on Sunday to try and meet a few people? I mean, how hypocritical is that when Mum doesn't even believe in God?'

'She believes in a creative force though,' I pointed out.

'That's not the same thing,' Bella argued.

I didn't think it was very different, but I decided to keep quiet because I didn't want to get drawn into an argument like the ones Bella is always having with Mum and Dad on just about every topic imaginable. She seems to make a point of disagreeing with other people these days, and she never even tries to phrase things tactfully like I would if I was contradicting someone.

'Did you know Aunt Thecla is taking us to buy our uniforms today?' I said, to change the subject. 'Mum was going to take us but now she's got some work stuff she needs to do.'

'More likely she's hoping Aunt Thecla will pay for everything,' Bella scoffed.

'*Shush* … she'll hear you,' I hissed.

'So?' Bella slid down to stand on the floor. 'She's probably expecting to have to buy our uniforms in any case. You do realise Dad's business hasn't been doing very well lately, don't you?'

I frowned. 'No.'

'Mum is stressing about money. She says she might have to go back to working full-time if things don't pick up. But you can't tell her I told you. I promised not to say anything, because she thinks you'll worry too much.'

Well, I will *now*, I felt like saying, wishing she wouldn't do this thing of telling me some secret that really *does* worry me, then forbidding me to talk about it to anyone, so my worry just gets even worse.

We were meant to be taking Grace with us to the shop so that Aunt Thecla could buy her uniform too, but when the time came Grace kicked up such a fuss that Mum gave in as usual and said she would take her later.

Lucky Grace. Or, as Bella would say, *clever* Grace.

It turned out that the lady who ran the uniform shop in the village – Mrs Mayhew – had grown up with our aunt. The two had lived within a few streets of each other all their lives, attended the same school and the same church, and now they sent each other Christmas cards and always stopped to speak in the street. But behind her back Aunt Thecla called Mrs Mayhew 'an awful snob' and 'a terrible gossip', and she said that she dreaded to think what Mrs Mayhew called *her*.

'You're frenemies!' Bella joked when Aunt Thecla described the situation to us. Then she had to explain to Aunt Thecla what a frenemy is.

As soon as we arrived at the shop, Mrs Mayhew greeted our aunt with a smile and then came forward to have a closer look at Bella and me. 'So, Thecla … these are Paul's girls, are they?'

'The older two – Bella and Elisabeth,' Aunt Thecla introduced us, quite proudly I thought. 'Girls, this is Valerie Mayhew.'

'Don't look much alike for sisters, do you?' Mrs Mayhew said as she looked us up and down in a way I found quite embarrassing. I wondered if she automatically sized people up for uniforms the second they walked into her shop. I just hoped she wasn't going to make some comment about our comparative measurements. I'm not fat but I'd really love to have Bella's measurements rather than mine. The fact is that Bella looks great in everything, whereas I have to be more careful what style of clothes to choose if I want to look good.

'Come this way, girls,' Mrs Mayhew said, waving us towards the changing rooms. 'I'll soon have you both kitted out.'

As we tried on our uniforms in separate changing rooms I pulled a face at myself in the mirror, wishing – yet again – that I looked more like my sister. I'd once told Aunt Thecla that I wished I looked as beautiful as Bella, and she said that I was beautiful too, just in a 'less obvious' way, whatever that was meant to mean. Actually, the more I thought about it the more I remembered other typically odd comments Aunt Thecla had made over the years, all aimed, I'm sure, at making me feel better about myself.

I heard Bella asking to try on a larger blouse, and then I heard Aunt Thecla's loud voice saying, 'I think we had better buy you a new bra as well. That one is looking rather grey. Your mother really ought to wash her whites separately, you know.'

Bella mumbled something I couldn't hear but I knew she was embarrassed.

'Don't be silly,' Aunt Thecla's voice came again.

'We're the only ones in the shop. Valerie, do you still sell underwear, or was that just while you had the boarders?'

'We haven't sold bras or knickers here for years, Thecla. Not since our day, I should think! Remember those navy-blue gym pants with a little pocket for your hanky?'

They both laughed and I knew Bella would be cringing as much as I was. It got worse though. 'If you want bras there's a very good shop in Castle Westbury, on the market square. I'd take them both there if I were you. No doubt your younger one will be needing something too? They like to wear them early these days, don't they? Makes them feel grown up.'

Now I was the one who felt mortified as they went on to discuss which other shops might sell good-quality trainer bras.

Suddenly there was a bit of a commotion outside my changing room and I pulled back my curtain to see what was happening. Bella had emerged fully dressed in her own clothes and was heading for the exit.

'BELLA, COME BACK AT ONCE!' our aunt was shouting after her.

'Sorry! I've got somewhere else I need to be!' Bella tossed back sharply as she barged out of the shop.

Aunt Thecla's face had gone pink. 'I do apologise, Valerie. I shall be having words with her later.'

'A bit of a rebel like her father, is she?' Mrs Mayhew commented slyly. 'You know, I was only thinking about your Paul the other day. I wonder how he feels about it all now.'

My ears pricked up at that. *Dad?* A *rebel?* What was she talking about?

'Valerie, can we save this for another time?' Aunt Thecla snapped, nodding across to where I was poking my head out from behind the curtain and staring at them.

'Oh, doesn't she know?' Mrs Mayhew sounded surprised.

'Good grief, Elisabeth, aren't you changed into that uniform yet?' Aunt Thecla asked swiftly. 'Come on! Quick sticks! I'd rather like to get at least *one* of you kitted out today.'

Chapter Nine

When we got back to Aunt Thecla's house, Dad was there with Grace. Aunt Thecla had hardly spoken to me on our way home, and when I'd asked her what Mrs Mayhew had meant by her comment about Dad she told me I'd have to ask him.

'Good news,' Dad greeted us with a smile. 'We've found a great little house to rent a couple of streets away from here and we can move in immediately.' He showed me a photo on his phone. 'Since it's unfurnished, we can get all our stuff out of storage as well.'

'Where's Bella?' Grace asked.

'Gone off in a strop,' Aunt Thecla said. 'Why don't you and the girls go out and look for her, Paul? No need to rush back. Frankly, I could do with a breather from all of you.'

Once we were outside I waited for Dad to stop complaining about how cringingly honest our aunt has always been before telling him some of what had happened in the shop. 'She really embarrassed us, Dad. I don't blame Bella for walking out.'

'She's not picking up,' Dad grunted as he tried to call Bella.'

'Dad … Mrs Mayhew said you were a rebel,' I said. 'How come?'

There was a pause as he put his phone away. Dad looked a bit put out. 'Valerie always was a stirrer.'

'So it's true then! But what did you *do*?'

He seemed to be avoiding my gaze as he said, 'Perhaps she meant I rebelled against my father … I also got into a bit of trouble with our next-door neighbour. It was his son Michael who was engaged to your aunt.'

'Really?' I was so interested in that piece of news that I was totally distracted from the story about Dad. 'So what happened? Why didn't they get married?'

'Michael's parents didn't approve and I think they put a lot of pressure on him to break it off.'

'*Why* didn't they approve?' I asked curiously.

'Michael was supposed to be studying for his A levels. They had high hopes that he'd get into Oxford or Cambridge, and they thought his romance with Thecla would be a distraction.'

64

'Poor Aunt Thecla! She must have been really upset.'
My mind was working overtime putting two and two
together. 'Is that the reason she's never married, do you
think? Because she never got over losing Michael?'

'Oh … well … I don't know –'

'Look, Daddy! There's Bella!' Grace suddenly
exclaimed, tugging his arm.

Sure enough, my older sister was walking towards us
carrying a large shopping bag.

'BELLA!' Dad immediately turned his full attention
her way. 'Where have you been?'

'Jeez, Dad, chill a minute!' Bella responded, scowling
at him under her long eyelashes. She'd put mascara on, I
noticed. Lipstick too. 'I just went for a walk.'

'Rather dressed up for a walk, aren't you?' Dad
growled.

She shrugged. 'Didn't know who I might meet.'

'Who *did* you meet?' he asked suspiciously.

Bella didn't bat an eyelid as she answered, 'Well,
one person was the lady who works in the post office.
She was very chatty … asked if Aunt Thecla had heard
the news about someone called Michael Godwin. He's
moving back to the village apparently, into his father's
old house.'

'Michael's back?' Dad let out a little gasp.

I instantly knew that it must be the same Michael. 'Oh wow!' I blurted.

'Why *wow*? Who is he?' Bella asked impatiently.

'Aunt Thecla used to be engaged to him,' I told her. 'He lived next door to Dad and her when they were children.'

Bella frowned. 'How come *you* know all this and I don't?'

Before I could answer Dad said sarcastically, 'Maybe because she actually hangs out with her family from time to time, Bella.'

When he asked her where else she'd been, she shrugged. 'Nowhere in particular. I just needed a break from Aunt Thecla and her gossipy pal. They really embarrassed us in that shop, didn't they, Libby?'

I nodded my agreement, suddenly feeling a strong yearning to be back on the same side as Bella – her and me against the grown-ups – the way life used to be when we were younger.

'It was *really* humiliating, Dad!' I said. 'They were going on about underwear and stuff in these really loud voices. It was horrible!'

Dad winced. 'All right. Enough. I believe you.' He took

hold of Grace's hand. 'Come on, Gracie. I'll take you to the swings before we go and meet Mummy from work.'

As Bella and I watched them go she grunted, 'Anyway, Aunt Thecla's the one who needs advice about bras. Have you *seen* that thing she's got drying on the clothes line today?'

And we both burst out laughing.

Chapter Ten

Over the next few days we gradually settled into our new house, which was only a street away from the dental practice where Mum was going to work. Mum took Bella and Grace to get their new uniforms, and Bella said that when she'd asked Mum if she'd managed to get Aunt Thecla to pay for them, Mum had looked a bit embarrassed and told her to keep her voice down.

I still had to share a bedroom with Bella, while Grace took the small single room that just about fitted her cabin bed. I'd always had my own room before. Even when Bella and I were younger we'd never had to share (apart from on holiday). I was a bit surprised by how big a deal it was not to have my own private space. I tried to cheer up by telling myself that sharing a room might bring us closer. Though in the cottage and at our aunt's house Bella had mostly turned her back on me and started texting Sam the second she'd climbed into bed. The only time that changed was if we had something particularly interesting to talk about. Or someone particularly interesting.

'I can't imagine Aunt Thecla being in love when she was eighteen, can you?' I said in a conspiratorial whisper as we lay in bed on our second night in our new bedroom. Our aunt's doomed engagement was something I'd always felt curious about, but now that we were living so close to her I was even more eager to know the whole story.

'I can't even imagine her *being* eighteen!' Bella replied with a smirk, turning to face me.

I giggled and so did she. It was then that she lowered her voice and said in her friendliest and most confiding tone, 'Listen, Libby ... I really need your help.'

I swear I actually felt a tingle of pleasure go up the back of my neck. (And yes, I do know that's pretty pathetic.)

'I need you to cover for me tomorrow with Mum and Dad,' she whispered. 'With Dad mainly ... you know how he fusses like an old granny about where I am.'

It's true that Dad tends to fret about Bella's whereabouts a lot more than Mum does. And he's always completely unapologetic when Bella accuses him of stifling her freedom, saying he doesn't care about that so long as she stays safe.

'Where are you going?' I asked suspiciously. Much as I longed to please her, I didn't want to commit to anything before I knew the details – especially not something that would get me into trouble.

She immediately went all cool on me again. 'Look, if you don't want to help, then just say so.'

'No, I do want to help!' In that moment I realised I was willing to sacrifice just about anything to feel like I mattered to her again.

She softened a bit then. 'Listen, I can't tell you where I'm going because it's better for you to genuinely not know if Mum or Dad ask you … you know how rubbish you are at lying … but hopefully they won't even find out I'm missing.' She paused. 'I promise I wouldn't ask you if it wasn't really important, Libby.'

Having her confide in me like this made me feel all warm and happy inside, just like I'd felt when we were younger and she'd included me in her life all the time.

'OK,' I said quickly. 'I'll cover for you.'

'Brilliant! This is what I need you to do …' And she got out of bed and came and sat down beside me, allowing her leg to actually *touch* mine as she outlined her plan.

70

* * *

The following morning, as Mum was about to leave the house for her first day at work, I announced that Bella and I were going out for a bike ride.

Dad looked up in surprise. 'Really? It looks like rain to me.'

'It's meant to get brighter as the day goes on,' Bella lied. 'Anyway, we've got waterproofs.'

'Where are you thinking of going?' Mum asked. 'These country roads can be quite dangerous for cyclists, you know. If a car comes round a bend and –'

'It's OK, Mum. There's a good cycle path alongside the river,' Bella said. 'I went down there to have a look the other day.'

Luckily Dad nodded his agreement. 'We used to use the river path a lot when I was young. It goes on for miles. Maybe Grace and I should come with you. We could have a proper family outing.'

'Not a good idea, Dad,' Bella said quickly.

'Why?' He sounded a bit suspicious and Bella looked like she was struggling to come up with a good answer.

That's when I had my brainwave. 'Because we haven't done anything, just the two of us, for ages,' I said, looking at Mum for support. Of course she immediately got on

71

board. She knows how rejected by Bella I've been feeling lately.

'Let them go, Paul. They'll have a better time on their own,' Mum said firmly. 'Why don't you take a picnic, girls?'

'You'll be lucky. There's hardly any bread left,' Dad said.

'Why don't you stop off at the baker's and get some rolls to take with you? I'll give you some money.'

'Cool. Thanks, Mum.' Bella actually went over and kissed her on the cheek. She hadn't done that in ages.

'Oh, and while you're out, can you pop into the uniform shop and see if the name labels we ordered are ready yet?'

'Sure, Mum. We'll collect them,' Bella said.

'Now, wish me luck for my first day.' Mum smiled as she picked up her umbrella to leave. 'Guess who's on my patient list this morning? Your headmistress, Mrs McLusky.'

'Mrs McLusky? Really?'

'She lives in the village,' Dad told us. 'You'll have to get used to bumping into people you know now that we live in a smaller community, girls.'

I wasn't sure I liked the idea of bumping into my teachers on a regular basis outside of school. And I certainly didn't like the idea of Mum being our head-mistress's dentist. 'What if Mrs McLusky has a really traumatic time getting a tooth pulled out or something?' I said after we'd waved Mum off. 'She might get horrible flashbacks every time she sees us in school. She's not going to like us very much then, is she?'

Dad laughed. 'Maybe you'll be a *good* reminder to go for all her check-ups and to keep her teeth in tip-top condition!'

'Don't be daft!' I said crossly.

After we'd got our bikes ready to go, Bella said she'd forgotten something. She dashed back into the house while I waited with the bikes. Then she came back to the front door with Dad hot on her heels. 'Just make sure you bring me some change from that!'

'Sure, Dad! If there is any!' she said cheekily.

'How expensive *are* these name tags?' he demanded, but Bella just grinned.

'See you later, Dad!' she called out.

Once we were away from the house, I said, 'But Mum already paid for the name tags.'

'Look, I need some extra cash, OK? Which is why I'm also keeping the money Mum gave me to buy our lunch.'

'What?!'

'Don't worry! I grabbed these ...' She stopped her bike abruptly to undo her rucksack. Inside she had stashed a whole packet of digestive biscuits, three apples, a big bag of raisins and a family-sized bag of crisps. She handed me the digestive biscuits and an apple. 'I'll meet you back here at five o'clock. But I'll text you first, OK?'

'Bella –'

'Thanks, Lib! I don't know what I'd do without you! Don't forget to pick up the labels!' And she gave me a quick hug and was gone.

For a few moments I stood feeling a bit of a warm glow inside, because for the first time in forever she had actually hugged me. But as I came out of my daze I started to feel less happy. What was I going to do all day on my own? The idea of a solitary bike ride along the river didn't exactly thrill me.

And where was Bella going? I thought about the money she'd taken with her – and the food. The raisins seemed an odd choice. Bella has never liked raisins much – not like Grace, who'll eat handfuls of them if you let her.

I decided I might as well pick up the labels anyway, so I headed for the uniform shop.

Inside the shop I saw that I wasn't the only customer. A tall man about the same age as my dad was speaking to Mrs Mayhew.

Suddenly a girl's cross voice sounded from behind the changing-room curtain. 'Dad, the skirt's really long.'

'Good,' said her father. 'Just stop complaining and show me, will you?'

'I haven't got the blouse on yet. I just can't believe we have to wear this archaic uniform!'

I gave a little cough to get Mrs Mayhew's attention. 'I've come to get our name labels,' I mumbled.

Mrs Mayhew looked me up and down then. 'Bella, isn't it?'

'Libby.' I felt like saying that she might remember if she looked at my face for more than two seconds.

'Ah, yes.' She turned to the man. 'Michael, this is Paul's daughter. Remember, I told you he's also just moved back. Libby, this is Mr Godwin, who used to live next door to your father.'

The man gave me a small smile. 'Hello.'

'Hello,' I muttered. I couldn't believe it. So *this* was the famous Michael Godwin – Aunt Thecla's former fiancé! He was tall and thin with grey hair and a very serious sort of face.

At that point a girl my age stepped out from the changing room dressed in the St Clara's uniform. She had short blonde hair, blue eyes and freckles. She was tall for her age and slim. I could instantly imagine her being brilliant at sports, unlike me.

'See what I mean? I look hideous!' she said stroppily, though in my opinion she looked much better than I did in the same uniform.

'Don't be silly. You look very smart. And you're going to need the blazer as well,' her dad said.

'Not the blazer! *Please*, Dad!'

'I'll compromise, but only if you stop fussing.'

'So if I stop fussing I don't have to get the blazer?' she asked hopefully.

'If you stop fussing I'll let you have the one that fits perfectly right now, rather than sizing up to one that will actually *last* you a couple of years.'

'Dad, that's so mean!' she protested.

'Tansy, this is Libby,' Mrs Mayhew introduced us swiftly. 'Libby is also starting in Year Eight at St Clara's. Isn't that nice?'

'Really?' She looked at me with new interest.

Mrs Mayhew handed me a bag of labels. 'Here you go, dear. I'm afraid three girls makes for a lot of name tags to sew on for your poor mum. Still … I'm sure your aunt will help.'

Was it my imagination or did she shoot a sly glance at Mr Godwin as she mentioned my aunt?

I'd already turned to leave the shop when Mr Godwin suddenly called out, 'How *is* Thecla?'

I swear I could feel the heat radiating off my face as I mumbled that she was fine. *No thanks to you*, I added inside my head, feeling oddly protective of my aunt. And yes, I do know their break-up happened a long time ago but that didn't change the fact that he had broken her heart – and she was probably the way she was now because of it.

Chapter Eleven

I couldn't wait to tell Bella about meeting Aunt Thecla's old fiancé, because I knew such juicy information was bound to earn me a good chunk of her undivided attention.

I found myself automatically following in the direction my sister had gone – up one of the side roads that led away from the river. I cycled to the end of the road and found a small car park next to a grassy area where a few younger kids were playing football. I couldn't see Bella but I spotted her bicycle chained up against some railings. I went over to inspect it just to make sure it was hers, then I walked into the field where the noisy ball game was going on. A girl who looked about my age was sitting on the grass.

'Hi,' I said shyly, walking up to her. 'I'm looking for my sister. That's her bike over there. Have you seen her?'

The girl looked up. 'She went off with some guy on a motorbike.'

'*What?*' I was totally shocked. 'Are you sure?'

She gave me a look like I was stupid and didn't bother to reply.

'Was it a young guy?' I asked, thinking that it had to be Sam, though I still wasn't quite able to believe it.

'Pretty young. Not some old pervert, if that's what's worrying you.' She was looking at me curiously. 'I haven't seen you here before.'

'We just moved here.'

'Oh yeah? I only moved here six months ago.'

'Really?' I was instantly interested, pleased to have found another newcomer.

I sensed she might be interested in me too. 'Are you starting at Westbury High?' she asked.

I shook my head. 'St Clara's.'

'Really?' She looked like she was about to say more, then suddenly tensed up as she spotted two girls our age walking towards us, dressed in jeans and branded T-shirts. They were carrying cans of Coke, and handed her one before flopping down on the grass beside her.

'Who's this then, Katie?' one of them asked. She was wearing quite a lot of make-up and she had a pink streak in her dark-blonde hair, which actually looked pretty cool.

'I've only just met her,' Katie replied. 'She's just moved into the village.'

'Hi, I'm Libby,' I said shyly.

'I'm Fran,' said the girl with the pink streak.

'I'm Lara,' said the other girl, who had long white-blonde hair and was very tall and slim. 'So are you going to Westbury High? What year are you in?'

Katie said, 'She's going to St Clara's.'

'OOH, Katie's got a friend at the posh school!' Fran teased.

'Don't be stupid,' Katie said crossly. 'She's looking for her sister. Remember that cute guy we saw on the motorbike?'

'*He's* her sister?' Lara said with a giggle. 'Wow – that's some amazing sex-change op!'

Fran started laughing too but Katie looked annoyed. 'The *girl* who got on his bike is her sister.'

'Her name's Bella,' I said, but none of them were listening to me.

Lara and Fran eventually stopped laughing. 'My dad says St Clara's is for girls who are too delicate or too dim to make it in a normal school,' Fran said.

'She doesn't *look* delicate,' Lara put in as she stared at me. 'At least her thighs certainly don't.'

'Right, so I guess that makes her dim!' Fran said, and they both started laughing their heads off again while Katie looked uncomfortable.

I could feel my face burning as I turned and walked away from them. So much for making friends here. I was relieved Bella wasn't with me because I know she's still really sensitive about other girls being bitchy – to me as well as to her. I was just really glad those three weren't going to the same school as us.

As soon as I was sure I was out of sight, I fished my phone out of my pocket to call my sister. I had other things to worry about now. Sam must have come here on his motorbike to visit her.

Her phone went straight to voicemail, so I sent her a text instead: *I know u r with Sam!*

A few minutes later she rang me. Before she could even speak I burst out, 'Bella, I know you're with Sam! I found your bike and someone saw you go off with him.'

'Libby, you haven't told Mum and Dad, have you?' She sounded breathless.

'Of course not!'

'Good. Listen, I'll explain everything when I get back. Just carry on with our plan for today. Promise me?'

'But –'

'Please, Libby? You're the only person I can trust … Listen, I have to go. I'll meet you where we said at five o'clock, OK?'

I didn't know what to do after she'd hung up, so I decided to chain my bike alongside hers and walk back to the high street.

No wonder Bella was being so secretive. If our parents found out Sam was here they'd kick up a massive stink. And if Dad found out she'd been riding around on Sam's motorbike … I shuddered as I thought back to the last row she'd had with Dad about Sam.

'I'm not a child any more, so stop interfering!' she'd shouted at him.

'You're fifteen!' Dad replied scornfully. 'You haven't got a clue what's best for you!'

'Dad, you are *so* patronising!' Bella retaliated, practically boiling with rage. 'You know what? One day I'm going to leave home with Sam and *never* come back, and you won't be able to do *anything* to stop us!'

I can't remember how Dad responded to that but I was pretty sure he hadn't taken her threat very seriously.

I thought about how Bella talks about Sam. It really isn't that dissimilar to the adoration she always seemed to have for Dad when we were younger. Everyone had called her a daddy's girl, just like they now call Grace a mummy's girl. It seems strange to imagine that now when you see how much Bella and Dad argue. She says he's stupidly overprotective and that he worries like an old woman – especially about us.

I was walking past the post office ten minutes later when I saw Tansy heading towards me. There was no sign of her dad.

'Hi,' I said, giving her a shy smile.

She immediately stopped to talk to me. 'It's Livvy, right?'

'Libby,' I corrected her. 'Short for Elisabeth.'

'Right.' Suddenly her attention was caught by something behind me. 'Look,' she said quietly. 'Isn't that Mrs McLusky?'

I turned to look. We were a short way along the road from the village dental practice and the headmistress of St Clara's was standing outside chatting to someone. And that someone was Aunt Thecla!

Of course it was no secret that they knew each other

but I still felt uncomfortable seeing them together. It felt like my aunt was encroaching on my school life, where she normally didn't belong.

Mrs McLusky was going inside the dentist's when Aunt Thecla turned her head and saw me. There was nothing for it but to wait for her to come over.

Suddenly Tansy's dad appeared beside us. 'Tansy – there you are!'

At first he didn't seem to recognise my aunt as she approached, but then he stiffened, standing almost to attention the nearer she got.

Aunt Thecla's eyesight obviously wasn't as good as his because she kept walking towards us with a smile on her face.

'Oh no,' I murmured under my breath. 'Please God …' The next thing I knew I was actually praying for divine intervention. I don't know quite what I expected God to do, but something along the lines of freezing time for a few minutes so that we could all run away would have been pretty good.

'Michael!' Aunt Thecla's voice was a little hoarse as she got close enough to recognise him.

'Hello, Thecla.'

They looked at each other so awkwardly that for

several moments it almost seemed that time really was standing still, waiting for one or the other of them to leg it out of there.

'Well, Michael,' my aunt finally said in a strange, tight voice. 'It's been a long time. How are you?'

'Good, thank you. Good enough anyway … You heard my father died?'

She nodded.

'I'm trying to sort out his house … I met um …' He glanced at me. Clearly he'd forgotten my name.

'Elisabeth and her two sisters are starting at St Clara's this year,' Aunt Thecla said as she looked questioningly at Tansy, who had drifted away to look in the bakery window.

'So is my daughter, Tansy,' he said. 'We've just been getting her uniform.'

Tansy turned round and my aunt let out a gasp of shock. 'Oh my goodness! She's the spitting image of –' She broke off, flushing pink and looking like she was worried she'd put her foot in it in some major way. 'Forgive me, Michael, I didn't mean to … I'm so clumsy sometimes …'

'Don't worry, Thecla,' he said at once. 'Anyway, it's true. She *does* take after him. Everybody who knew him says so.' He paused. 'As you can imagine, my father was absolutely delighted!'

She gave a weak smile. 'I *can* imagine.' There was an even longer awkward silence. 'Um … I was just going to get a coffee, so …'

'Actually, Thecla, perhaps I could join you?' he said in a rush.

Aunt Thecla looked totally floored. I could tell she hadn't seen that one coming. 'Well …'

'Here, Tansy.' Her dad swiftly handed her some money. 'Why don't you girls go and buy yourselves an ice cream?'

'So do you know anyone else here?' Tansy asked me as we sat down on the wooden bench in front of the village war memorial, licking the ice creams we'd just bought. I was keeping a lookout for the girls I'd met at the park, but thankfully there was no sign of them.

'No,' I replied, my friend radar switching on for the second time that morning. 'Do you?'

'Nope.'

Good, I thought. 'Where have you moved from?'

'Southampton. Now Grandpa's died my dad's decided to come back and live here. It's a crazy idea if you ask me.'

'Is it just you and your dad then?' I asked curiously.

'Yes. Mum and Dad are divorced, and I'm living with

Dad because Mum's gone to Africa to work for a charity there. She's a doctor and she's helping to set up a health clinic.'

'Wow.' I felt pleased that she was confiding in me so easily. Maybe Tansy wanted a new friend just as much as I did. 'So how long has she been away?' I asked, trying to sound politely interested rather than super-nosy. (Bella says I sometimes sound like I'm interrogating people when I get curious and want to know more.)

'Almost four months. It was meant to be three but it got extended. She gets back to England in two weeks' time though.'

'I bet you can't wait to see her.' I could only guess how much I'd miss Mum if she ever went away for that long.

When Tansy just shrugged rather than agreeing with me, I asked, 'So ... will your mum have to go away again after that or is she back for good?' Maybe her mum was leaving again and that was why she still seemed unhappy.

'No.' Tansy sounded angry as she added, 'But I'm still not going back to live with her. I don't care what she says!'

'Oh ...' I could sense there was more she wasn't telling me, but I didn't feel like I knew her well enough to ask without risking her thinking I was sticking my nose in.

We sat silently eating our ice creams while I tried to think of something else to say. If there's one thing I'm good at it's getting people to talk about themselves.

'So how do you like living in the country?' I finally asked.

She pulled a face. 'It sucks! I mean, Dad never really talks about growing up here, but as far as I can work out the most exciting thing that ever happened when he was a kid was the church fête!'

I smiled. 'Don't forget the annual tractor race!'

'Dad actually won that one year,' Tansy said with a grin. 'He and his girlfriend paid a local farmer to let them use his tractor. He says no one could believe it when they came first. He says it was all down to his girlfriend, because she drove like a maniac!'

I was positive that the girlfriend in question had to be Aunt Thecla. I couldn't imagine her perched on a tractor, but the driving like a maniac sounded right. And I was sure I'd also heard some story about her winning the village tractor race.

'Tansy, did you know that your dad and my aunt lived next door to each other when they were young? And that they were engaged for a while.'

'What? You mean that aunt we met just now?' she

looked shocked. Then she started to grin. 'Oh wow! I *thought* he was acting a bit weird. I had no idea *she* was Bluebell!'

'Bluebell?' I was confused. 'But that's not her name!'

'Oh, Bluebell was just Dad's pet name for her. Her real name was pretty weird apparently.'

'Thecla?' I said.

She grinned. 'Very possibly. Wow! I can't believe Bluebell is your aunt! Wait till I tell my mum. *She* thinks Dad never really got over his first love ... though Dad says that's rubbish!' She grinned even wider. 'I'm telling you, seeing him with your aunt just now, I'm thinking Mum might be right ... I've never seen him so keen to take someone out for coffee!'

Chapter Twelve

I was longing to tell Bella about Aunt Thecla being called Bluebell by Tansy's dad – and how Tansy thought he was still secretly in love with our aunt. I was pretty sure Bella was going to laugh her head off when she heard that. As for me, I didn't just find it funny, I found it totally thrilling. And if Tansy was right then this was something I couldn't just leave alone. I had to find out if Aunt Thecla might still be in love too. Of course on the surface she wasn't, but what about deep down? Buried so deep that nobody else would ever know? And what if the two of them could somehow be brought back together?

But first I had to find Bella and make her tell me what was going on with Sam.

I felt a bit nervous about going back to wait for her at the park because I really didn't want to meet those three girls again. Luckily there was no sign of them.

I didn't text Bella because I was imagining her on the back of Sam's bike and I figured it was safer for her to keep holding on rather than being distracted by her phone.

I spotted the motorbike straight away as it came down the street towards me. At least it wasn't roaring along at top speed, and I could see that Sam and my sister were both wearing helmets.

They stopped just in front of me and Bella immediately removed her helmet and shook out her hair. 'Libby.'

'Hi, Libby,' Sam echoed as he lifted his visor so I could see his face.

'I should have guessed *you* were the reason she was sneaking off all the time,' I told him coolly.

He looked a bit surprised by my unfriendliness.

'Shut up, Libby, this is nothing to do with you,' Bella said sharply. 'Sam, you'd better go. My aunt has spies everywhere in this village.'

I stared at him as he said goodbye, remembering how Katie and her friends had called him cute earlier. I have to say I've never really thought of Sam as cute, but then again there's definitely something quite striking about his face. He has brown eyes set in an angular face and a mop of messy dark-blond hair. Today he was wearing jeans, a leather jacket and big biker boots, and he looked tougher and more streetwise than usual.

'But, Bella, what's he *doing* here?' I burst out the second he'd driven off.

'Trying to find a job.'

'I thought he already had a job with his uncle!'

'He wants a job *here*, stupid … near *me*!'

'Wow! So does his mum know he's here?' Sam doesn't have a dad – at least not one who's ever been around – and his mum has always seemed extremely laidback and hands-off compared to my parents. But still …

'She knows he's OK,' Bella grunted. 'I don't think she cares beyond that.'

'So where's he staying?'

'At a B & B in the village. But he's run out of money, so after tonight he has to move somewhere else.'

Now I understood why she'd needed all that money. 'Bella, can't you just ask Mum and Dad to help? Maybe when they see how badly the two of you want to stay together …'

'Yeah … right …' she said sarcastically.

'But don't you think –?'

'Libby, we've already got it covered, OK? I'm going to take him to the cottage.'

'What cottage?'

'Rat Cottage, of course! It's still empty and there's that window at the back that doesn't shut properly, so it should be easy for him to sneak in and out.'

'But, isn't that against the law?' I asked in alarm.

'Probably.'

'So what if he gets caught? He'll get into loads of trouble.'

'We haven't got a choice. I've already given him all my savings *and* the money I managed to get off Dad this morning. He bought some food and some more petrol for his bike but there's nothing left.'

'But, Bella –'

'Libby, you have to promise not to say anything about this to anyone. If you do …' She spoke in a voice that told me that if I did I'd regret it.

'I won't tell,' I promised, instantly subdued by the threat of losing her trust again.

'I knew I could count on you.'

She quickly changed the subject by asking me what I'd been doing while she was gone. And as I'd expected, she was intrigued to learn that I'd met Michael Godwin and

Tansy. When I mentioned Aunt Thecla's nickname she laughed in disbelief. 'I mean, I can think of some other less delicate plant names that would suit her.'

'Like what?' I asked with a grin.

She shrugged. 'Thistle ... or *Cactus*!'

I laughed, even though I don't think our aunt is really all that prickly. Bossy and interfering, maybe. Though I guess Bella might have a different opinion. In any case, I didn't contradict her because it felt nice, the two of us laughing together like this. It made me feel like I was back on Team Bella.

'So did Mrs McLusky need any fillings?' Grace asked Mum as we all sat down together at the dinner table that evening.

'I should think Mummy is too bound by patient–dentist confidentiality to answer that question,' Dad said in a jokey sort of voice. 'Isn't that right, Nina?'

'Absolutely,' Mum said. 'Anyway, the last thing your poor headmistress needs is a lot of children standing in the playground gossiping about the state of her teeth.'

'Why? *Are* they in a bit of a state then?' Bella asked with a grin.

'They look in tip-top condition to me,' Dad responded, then realised his mistake when Mum frowned at him.

'Since when did *you* get such a close look at her teeth?'

Dad instantly held up both hands in a 'Don't shoot!' kind of way. 'Yours are looking even more tip-top, Nina.'

'*And* they're a hundred per cent real!' Mum said tartly.

'Wait … are you saying Mrs McLusky's teeth *aren't* real?' Bella and I both blurted, which made Dad snort and Mum's mouth twitch, though she still managed not to grin.

'Aunt Thecla had *really* nice teeth when she was young,' Grace announced suddenly. 'She showed me a big photo of her face. I didn't know it was her at first, because she looked so pretty.'

'Now there's a crumpliment if ever there was one!' Dad said with a mischievous grin.

Just then the doorbell rang.

'That's Aunt Thecla,' Grace said. 'She said she was coming round after dinner to see where we've hung up all her paintings.'

'WHAT?' Mum and Dad both nearly choked on their food. 'Grace, why didn't you tell us?'

My little sister looked indignant. 'I just *did*!'

'I'm not putting any of them up,' Mum exclaimed. 'Not one!'

Dad nodded. 'Don't worry, Nina. Just leave it to me.'

The following morning as Bella and I were still lazing in bed, I said, 'So do you think Aunt Thecla believed Dad about the box with her paintings in it being permanently lost in storage?'

'Nope.'

'Neither do I. She took it pretty well though, don't you think?'

'Offering to paint us some more? I'm telling you, the next ones she gives us are going to be even more hideous.'

I smiled. After a short silence I said, 'I wish she wasn't looking after us today.' Dad was away meeting a client for most of the day and Mum had been asked at the last minute if she could go in on her day off to cover a sick colleague's caseload. Aunt Thecla had offered to help out.

'She's not going to be looking after *us* – just Gracie,' Bella said firmly. 'And I think it's quite handy that Dad won't be here. It's always easier to see Sam when he's not around.'

Aunt Thecla arrived half an hour after Dad had left, just as Mum was setting off to walk to work. Once she'd gone, Bella announced that she was going out on her bike to get some fresh air. Aunt Thecla is a big fan of fresh air, especially country air. She also never bats an eyelid (like Mum and Dad do) when one of us tells her we want to be on our own for a while. She thinks it's perfectly normal to need time away from other human beings.

Bella left while I was up in our bedroom getting dressed, and when I came downstairs Aunt Thecla was complaining about the lack of fresh food in the house. I thought she was exaggerating because I knew Dad had stocked up at the supermarket before he left, but when I opened the fridge I saw what she meant. The bread bin was empty too.

I was pretty sure I knew where all the food had gone.

Grace suddenly asked, 'Can we bake something, Aunt Thecla?'

'I very much doubt we have sufficient ingredients,' she replied. 'But we can buy some if we go to the shops. Now then … let's make a list.'

'I'm going out on my bike for a bit,' I announced. 'I've got my phone with me. I'm going to try and catch up with Bella.'

'Didn't she just say she wanted to be alone?' Aunt Thecla called out after me, but I pretended I hadn't heard as I shut the door behind me.

I knew – or at least I *thought* I knew – exactly where Bella was going. So when she didn't answer her phone or my text asking where she was I didn't let that stop me.

It felt like forever but in fact it only took twenty minutes to cycle to our old cottage – Rat Cottage as we all referred to it now.

There was no sign of anyone in the two neighbouring cottages, though a car was parked on the grass verge in front. I couldn't see my sister's bicycle or Sam's motorbike anywhere, but it made sense that they'd have hidden them.

I propped up my bike against the side of the cottage and crept round the back to find the dodgy window. Nothing had changed. The grass was still overgrown and judging by the droppings on the patio the rats were still alive and kicking. Even the Frisbee Grace had managed to get stuck in the tree was still up there.

Suddenly footsteps behind me made me jump and as I turned a familiar voice said, 'Hey! It's Libby, isn't it? What are *you* doing here?'

It was the girl I'd met at the park – Katie. I was so stunned to find her here that I couldn't speak at first. I soon recovered enough to mumble, 'We used to rent this cottage. That's our Frisbee.' I pointed a bit lamely up at the tree.

'Wait – was it *your* family who upset Mrs Fuller so badly?' She sounded amused.

'She upset *us*!' I protested. 'That house is disgusting inside!' I paused. 'But how come *you're* here?'

'My aunt and uncle live next door. They're going on holiday today so we're giving them a lift to the station. You're lucky they already took the dogs to the kennels this morning. If the dogs had found you here they might have got nasty.'

'Yeah … well … the dogs actually shouldn't be in this garden,' I murmured, edging past her to get back round to the front,

'That's what my mum says. My auntie doesn't like Mrs Fuller though, so I don't think she cares.'

I could feel Katie's eyes on me, watching as I collected my bicycle. I was trying to think of something friendlier to say. On her own Katie seemed OK, although I was still wary of her two friends.

It was then that I heard voices and saw Bella and Sam walking round the bend in the road.

'Libby, what are you doing?' Bella called out crossly. 'Does Aunt Thecla know you're here? You're going to spoil everything if you're not careful –'

'Hey!' Sam came to the rescue, giving my sister a sharp

nudge as he spotted Katie standing silently behind me watching us. 'Who's this then, Libby?' he asked, trying to sound calm though I could tell he was nervous.

'This is Katie,' I introduced her quickly. 'Her aunt and uncle live in the middle cottage.'

Suddenly we heard a door opening and adult voices talking and laughing. A man and a woman emerged from the middle cottage carrying suitcases.

'Come on, Libby. Let's go,' Bella said sharply.

'See you around, Libby,' Katie called out.

My legs felt like they were made of lumps of wood as I hurried back along the road with Bella and Sam. When we were finally out of sight of the cottage, Bella turned and glared at me. 'Are you *trying* to get us caught?'

I glared back. 'I was just trying to find you, that's all! Where were you?'

'We were hiding my bike in the woods,' Sam said, putting a reassuring hand on her shoulder. 'Did Bella tell you about the den we found? We've patched it up and it makes a pretty good shelter.'

And a pretty good place to roll around snogging, I thought. Though of course I didn't dare say that.

'Come on, Libby,' Sam said. 'Come and see it. It's actually pretty cool.'

Chapter Thirteen

'This *is* cool,' I said when I set eyes on it.

They'd first discovered the abandoned den while we'd been living at the cottage, when Bella had already been meeting up with Sam in secret. Apparently he'd driven here the day after we had. The den was made under a low overhanging tree, using lots of broken-off branches propped up and wedged into place to make slanting walls. Sam had found an old sheet of plastic in a skip, which he'd used to cover part of the roof.

Inside the shelter was all Sam's stuff, including his motorbike. Bella's bicycle was leaning up against it.

'I'm still a bit worried about leaving my bike here for too long,' he said. 'Whoever made this den might come back, and I don't fancy a load of kids crawling over it or someone siphoning off my petrol. I think I should stay here at night, Bella, at least for now.'

'Don't be daft. You should totally make use of the cottage. It's not like you'll be doing any damage.'

'But it's still against the law.'

'Well, you won't get caught,' Bella said firmly. 'Especially now that the people next door are going away.'

'Katie told me the dogs went to the kennels this morning,' I said.

'See!' said Bella. 'And the old lady in the third cottage is deaf and never answers her door, so she won't be any trouble.'

'All the same, I think I'll sleep out here tonight,' Sam said stubbornly.

'You do realise that the weather forecast is really bad for this weekend, don't you?' I said. 'There's supposed to be a storm, and it's not safe to shelter underneath trees if there's thunder and lightning. You could get electrocuted.'

Bella looked at me gratefully as he sighed and said, 'If the weather's bad I'll sleep in the cottage. But really I just want to find some work so I can move back to the B & B.'

As we headed back towards civilisation my phone rang. The three of us had just reached the road where the trees ended and Sam was about to ride off to the jobcentre in Castle Westbury. I checked to see who was calling me and wished I hadn't when I saw that it was Aunt Thecla.

'Don't answer it,' Bella said.

'I have to,' I grunted.

Thankfully it was Grace at the other end. 'Libby, we've just put our cakes in the oven,' she told me excitedly. 'And now Aunt Thecla wants to give me an art lesson. Oh … and a girl called in to see you.'

'What girl?'

'Tansy. Aunt Thecla called her Pansy and she got really cross.' She giggled. 'She was going somewhere on the bus and she came to see if you wanted to go with her.'

'Going *where* on the bus?'

'Shopping. In a castle.'

'*Castle?* Oh, do you mean Castle Westbury?'

I could hear our aunt saying something in the background, then Grace said, 'Aunt Thecla wants to know where you are.'

'With Bella. We'll be home soon.'

As I came off the phone, Sam said, 'I can give you a lift to Castle Westbury if you like.'

'What? On that thing?' I had butterflies in my tummy just at the thought of riding on his motorbike.

'Hey, I'm a perfectly safe driver, you know,' he said indignantly as he fastened his helmet.

'Don't take it personally,' Bella said. 'Dad's completely brainwashed her about motorbikes.'

I averted my eyes as they kissed goodbye.

After Sam had gone, Bella and I cycled back to the village together, with Bella barking, 'Car!' whenever she heard one approaching. And instead of feeling annoyed every time she yelled at me to keep closer to the hedge, I found myself feeling pleasantly surprised by how protective she was being.

We arrived back to find Aunt Thecla in the kitchen with Grace, showing her how to draw pictures using charcoal.

'Girls, I need one of you to go to my house and fetch me some hairspray,' she greeted us. 'I need it to set the charcoal on these drawings or they'll smudge. I've looked upstairs but your mother doesn't seem to have any.' She sounded a bit irritated by that fact.

'Yeah, well, only old ladies use hairspray these days,' Bella muttered.

'I'll go,' I offered hastily.

'I'll come with you,' Bella said, ignoring our aunt's glare.

Once we reached the house I realised why Bella had

wanted to come. 'I'm going to see what food she's got in her kitchen,' she told me.

'Don't take too much,' I warned her as I hurried up to the bathroom where Aunt Thecla usually kept her hairspray.

When I couldn't find any, I decided to look in her bedroom instead. I'd glimpsed inside her bedroom before while we'd been staying here, but she usually kept the door closed and we weren't allowed to go in without her permission. Also off limits was her art studio, though she never took any chances with that, keeping it locked the whole time we were there.

Now I had the opportunity to look around her bedroom properly I noticed that it was the lightest, most colourful room in the house. It had three bold abstract paintings on one wall, which were her own work, and which I liked a lot more than any of the paintings she'd ever given us. I looked on her dressing table for hairspray but I couldn't see any.

The top drawer of the dressing table was partly open and I could see loose photos and what looked like a couple of small photo albums inside. Of course I knew I should close the drawer immediately but I was far too curious.

I carefully slid out a small black leather album. To my

surprise it was filled with photographs of me and my sisters as babies. I returned it to the drawer and took out an envelope containing some older-looking colour photos. They were of Aunt Thecla as a girl of perhaps seventeen or eighteen. In one picture she was sitting in a field of bluebells. In another I hardly recognised her because her hair was loose – a rich dark-brown colour, flowing in waves down her back. In that one she wore a blue summer dress and she was balancing on the branch of a tree. There was another of her pulling a silly face, and another of her waving to the camera. I was surprised to see what an attractive young woman she had been.

Lastly there was a photo of a young man standing in the same field of bluebells, blowing a kiss to whoever was holding the camera (presumably Aunt Thecla?). I studied the young man's face to see if it resembled Michael Godwin's. I couldn't really tell, but then I noticed the writing on the back of the photograph:

A kiss for my Bluebell, with love from M

'WOW!' I said out loud. I could feel butterflies in my chest, a mix of nerves and excitement. I felt like I'd found a clue in some huge and tantalising mystery.

106

'Wow, *what?*' Bella asked from the doorway.

I instantly wished that Tansy was here instead of Bella. I had a feeling Tansy might actually share a bit of my excitement.

'You *do* know Aunt Thecla would kill you if she knew you were going through her stuff, don't you?' Like I already said, Bella isn't nearly as curious as I am about other people and she's always saying I'm way too nosy.

I hurriedly replaced the photos in the drawer. 'I'm still looking for the hairspray,' I said, although I couldn't have cared less about finding that now. All I wanted to do was search through the rest of my aunt's stuff to find more clues.

'Oh, I already found that in the kitchen. Come on.'

I suppose I should have been grateful that she was forcing me to leave before my curiosity got the better of me. I can so relate to the saying that curiosity killed the cat. You wouldn't think curiosity could be so dangerous but, believe me, sometimes it can pretty much choke to death any sense you've got and make you behave in a way that's just plain wrong.

Sitting ready by the front door was a large carrier bag of food. 'Bella, you can't take all that!'

'It's OK. It's all stuff from the back of her cupboards. She won't notice – at least not for a while.' She shoved the can of hairspray into my hand and told me to take it to our house. 'I'm going to stash this lot at the cottage for Sam.'

Chapter Fourteen

The next few days were very busy. Dad was working from home and Mum was working full-time at her new dental practice because one of the other dentists was off sick. Bella was spending most of her time with Sam.

He'd been sleeping in the cottage for the past few days, ever since the weather had worsened. It had basically been raining non-stop, and as he hadn't had any luck finding a job he was feeling pretty miserable.

'Couldn't he sell his motorbike if he needs money?' I suggested to Bella.

'Of course not. He'd be stranded without it. Besides, he loves that bike.'

'But he hasn't even got money to buy petrol,' I pointed out.

'I found some more money for him. It's enough for fuel and food for a while. And he should be safe enough in the cottage, especially with the neighbours away.'

'Where did you get the extra money?' I asked, puzzled.

At first I thought she wasn't going to tell me, then she shrugged as if she didn't see the point in hiding it.

'You know Aunt Thecla has that tin on the shelf in her kitchen? Well, the other day when we went round to get the hairspray I had a look inside. It's stuffed with money – I counted almost a hundred pounds. I took some of that.'

'Bella, that's *stealing*!' I was horrified.

'It's *borrowing*. I'll put it back at some point. In any case, Aunt Thecla doesn't need it – she has loads of money. She probably won't even notice it's gone.'

I frowned, struggling to feel comfortable with this. 'I guess I could try and think of it like Robin Hood,' I murmured, 'stealing from the rich to give to the poor ...'

'I don't care how you think of it,' said Bella with a dismissive shrug. 'Just don't tell Sam where the money came from. He's feeling guilty enough about still owing his uncle loads of money for his bike.'

I sighed. 'Taking money from Aunt Thecla just feels really wrong, that's all.'

'Yeah, well, blame Dad, not me.'

'Huh?'

'He's the one who's backed me into this corner. If he wasn't so mean about Sam, we could just ask *him* for help.'

I pulled a face, which I guess must have expressed how I felt about her logic.

She instantly glared at me and went all defensive. 'It's *true*,' she snapped.

I didn't respond. I actually thought that blaming Dad for what she'd done was a huge cop-out, not to mention totally ludicrous, but needless to say I wasn't brave enough to tell her that.

The next day as she was leaving for work Mum said, 'I've got Tansy Godwin coming for an appointment this afternoon. You three haven't had check-ups in a while, so you may as well come in today too.'

'Do we have to, Mum?' Bella complained. I knew she'd been planning on meeting up with Sam that afternoon.

'Yes. I've got some free time after Tansy. You can all come down to the surgery at four o'clock. It shouldn't take long.'

'How do you know it won't take long?' Bella grunted huffily. 'We might need loads of fillings.'

'You'd better not,' Mum said. 'And you'd better all be on your best behaviour in that waiting room today, or else!' She glared at Bella and me. 'That means no chatting about long needles and loud drills and dentists pulling out teeth with pliers!'

Bella and I started laughing, remembering the visit she was talking about when we'd got a bit bored waiting for her.

'It's not funny!' Mum snapped. 'Two of my clients complained, and there was a little boy who was so scared he wouldn't open his mouth when his mother brought him in. I didn't dare tell her you were anything to do with me.'

'Mum, we're never going to do that again,' I said, pulling myself together when I saw how cross she was.

'I'm very glad to hear it!' she said, not seeming very glad at all as she slammed the front door behind her.

'Oh dear,' I murmured guiltily.

But Bella just sounded impatient as she said dismissively, 'Honestly, it was more than a year ago! You'd really think she'd be over that by now!'

Bella and I went to collect Grace from Aunt Thecla's house that afternoon before our dental appointment.

She'd told us to come early because she had a surprise for us.

'I bet it's another painting,' Bella said as we set off. 'It'll be something even more hideous this time – you'll see!'

Aunt Thecla had been spending a lot more time with Grace ever since she'd decided that Grace showed 'artistic potential'. I have to confess I was a little hurt by her newfound favouritism. Previously I had always been the one she paid most attention to, mainly because she thought I was the clever one. (I've always had better marks than Bella in all my exams, though I think that's probably because she never does any work, whereas I always study really hard.)

'Grace is in the kitchen having a little snack before she goes,' our aunt told us when we arrived. 'I know one normally doesn't eat before a visit to the dentist, but as it's only your mother …' She trailed off as if it went without question that Mum wouldn't mind.

I was about to point out that if the snack was anything Mum might have to pick out of Grace's teeth before she could examine them properly, then she probably *would* mind, but before I could speak, Aunt Thecla was ushering us into the kitchen.

113

On the table lay four different photographs of blue-bells and four matching pastel pictures.

'Guess which is mine,' Grace challenged us through a mouthful of cheese sandwich.

Now you'd think it would be obvious which picture had been drawn by a six-year-old, but it actually wasn't. The pictures were all much better than anything I could have done. In the end Grace couldn't contain herself any longer. 'They're *all* mine!' she squealed.

'No way! That's brilliant, Grace!' I exclaimed.

She giggled in delight while our aunt smiled proudly at her.

'Bluebells were Aunt Thecla's favourite flower when she was a little girl,' Grace said, like she was announcing a very important historical fact.

I made the connection then. 'Wait, is *that* why Tansy's dad called you Bluebell?'

My aunt looked flummoxed for several seconds. 'And how would you know about that?' she finally asked in a very guarded sort of voice.

'Tansy told me,' I replied, not seeing why she should be ashamed of it.

Aunt Thecla was glaring at me. 'What else did she tell you?'

I blushed. 'Nothing really. I mean, I only know that you and Tansy's dad were engaged when you were young.'

'We were *very* young,' Aunt Thecla added, in a tone suggesting that in her opinion 'very young' and 'very foolish' went hand in hand. 'And, yes, the boys called me Bluebell – not that it matters any more.' Her tone became softer. 'Now … while I have the three of you here, I have something to give you all.' She headed for the living room, clearly expecting us to follow.

'Here we go,' Bella muttered under her breath, but as we entered the room Aunt Thecla gestured towards the coffee table, where we saw three sparkling brooches.

'They're diamond brooches that belonged to my mother,' she explained. 'After your grandfather died I found them in his safe. There was a note with them, asking me to give one each to you three girls.'

'I want this one!' Grace burst out excitedly, rushing to grab one, while Bella and I just stood back in silent awe.

'I thought you'd like that greyhound brooch, Grace,' our aunt said. 'It's set with diamonds but it has a ruby eye and ruby collar … and I thought the bird of paradise would be perfect for you, Bella. Quite beautiful and exotic, don't you think?'

She handed it to Bella, who gently ran her fingers over the diamond-studded body and the ruby and emerald detail in the tail. I could tell that she loved it.

'Libby, I thought you would like the bumblebee. Very quirky and unusual, don't you agree?' She handed the last brooch to me. Its body was set with diamonds but unlike the other two it was finished with dainty black enamel stripes.

'It's beautiful, Aunt Thecla. Thank you,' I said as Grace made her doggy brooch leap about on the coffee table.

'I've had them valued and each brooch is worth around five thousand pounds,' she told us matter-of-factly.

'Five *thousand*?' I thought she must be joking at first. Come to think of it, even if she'd said five *hundred* pounds I'd have thought she was joking.

'Yes. The bee one is possibly a bit less valuable but it's always been my favourite. We kept bees for a while when I was a child, you know. Once, when your dad was about ten or eleven, he decided to try and steal some of their honey. He covered up well and used gloves but he didn't think about his face. The bees got in plenty of stings, I'm afraid.'

'Poor Dad,' I said sympathetically.

'Yes. And after our father got through with him I don't know what stung more – his face or his bottom,' she added drily.

'That is so mean!' I burst out.

'Well, it was almost forty years ago and your grandfather had quite old-fashioned ideas about raising children even then.'

'Dad says Grandpa was a horrible father,' I said.

She let out a sad sigh. 'I think if our mother had been able to support him more – rather than being sick and needing his help a lot of the time – then things might have been different. But, yes, your dad didn't have an easy time growing up. Our father was harder on him than on me, I think mainly because he was a boy.'

'Come on, Libby!' Bella said impatiently. She's never as interested in hearing about the past as I am. 'We have to leave now.'

I ignored her, longing to hear more about Dad as a boy and to find out what Mrs Mayhew had meant when she'd called him a rebel.

But Aunt Thecla seemed to pull herself back to the present as she said, 'Yes, we'd better get you to the dentist. Just because it's only your mother it doesn't mean we should be late.'

117

Chapter Fifteen

Tansy and her dad were still in the waiting room when we got there, which meant Mum must be running late.

'Hi, Libby,' Tansy greeted me at once.

'Hi, Tansy,' I said with a grin, feeling pleased to be welcomed in such a friendly manner.

Aunt Thecla looked less pleased, however. In fact, she sounded particularly awkward as she said hello.

I sat down across from Tansy's dad so that I could sneak a better look at him, trying to compare him to that photograph I'd found. I was dying to tell Tansy about it but I knew this wasn't the right time.

Tansy's dad cleared his throat and seemed like he was about to say something. Aunt Thecla looked across at him expectantly, but then he seemed to change his mind.

'We've been waiting *ages*,' Tansy said conversationally. 'We were supposed to go in half an hour ago.'

'Well, I'm sure there's a perfectly good reason,' Aunt Thecla snapped, her haughty side coming out in defence of Mum.

I felt embarrassed, since I was pretty sure Tansy hadn't meant to be critical. Before I could think of something to say to smooth things over Grace did the job for me.

'Mummy says it's never her fault if she's running late,' she said earnestly. 'It's always because of a difficult patient or a difficult tooth.'

Tansy grinned and her dad let out a laugh. 'Well, at least we haven't heard any screams coming from inside,' he said.

Aunt Thecla gave a little laugh to match his.

Grace was looking at Aunt Thecla curiously. 'From now on I'm going to call you Aunt Bluebell!' she suddenly announced.

Our aunt immediately sobered up. 'Don't be silly, Grace.'

'But it's a really pretty name. And *you're* really pretty when you laugh.'

Aunt Thecla blushed and Bella and I glanced at each other, not knowing whether to laugh or squirm.

'Tansy, would you like to go through now?' the receptionist said.

As Tansy stood up so did her dad. 'I want to have a chat about whether or not you need braces.'

'Mum said I don't have to!'

'I know, but she's a doctor not a dentist. I want a second opinion.'

As they left the waiting area Bella whispered to me, 'Sam thinks *he* needs braces.'

Unfortunately our aunt overheard. '*Sam*? Isn't that the boy you had all the problems with?'

Bella scowled. '*Dad* was the only one with a problem.'

I expected Aunt Thecla to jump to Dad's defence, but surprisingly she just looked thoughtful as she asked, 'A bit overprotective, was he?'

'More like a *lot* overprotective! And a lot over-interfering *and* overbearing!' Bella declared with feeling.

Aunt Thecla nodded as if she understood. 'Well, he's always been overprotective of the people he cares about. If he was like it with me when we were young, I'm sure he must get terribly upset when any of *you* three try anything too adventurous.'

'Did he try and stop *you* from doing stuff then?' I asked curiously. 'Even though you were older than him?'

'Anything he thought risky, yes. I think it was because our mother had died and he was terrified of losing me

120

too. Of course I had no understanding of that back then. There was only one time when he interfered and caused something dreadful to happen as a result –' She broke off abruptly as Tansy's dad came back into the waiting room alone and told the receptionist he was just popping outside for some fresh air while he waited for Tansy.

'Well, Libby ... Bella ...' Aunt Thecla said. 'I'm sure you two can keep an eye on Grace until your mother is ready for you.' And she promptly left too. Through the window we could see her chatting to Tansy's dad.

As soon as it was just the three of us, Bella whispered to me that she was going to meet Sam the moment her check-up was done. 'Cover for me when you get home, OK?'

'How?' I protested.

'I don't know. Tell them I went for a walk. Say I wanted some time on my own to think.'

I rolled my eyes, imagining how well that explanation was going to go down. Meanwhile, I couldn't stop thinking about what Aunt Thecla had just let slip about Dad. He'd certainly never told *us* about any catastrophe he'd caused as a boy, so what was she talking about? I found myself wondering if Tansy knew anything about it. After all, it was possible that her dad might have told her something. I decided that when she came back into the waiting room I was going to try and arrange a time for the two of us to meet up.

I won't bother describing my hideous dental check-up, but just imagine a normal dental appointment, minus the usual politeness.

'Open your mouth wider, Libby!'

'*Aaa ...*'

'I thought you said you'd been flossing?'

'*Aaa ... haa ...*'

'Not well enough, young lady! Look at all this tartar.'

Mum shoved the end of her metal probe under my nose to show me the bit of yellow gunk she'd scraped off. Then she went on about how I can't afford to be lazy when it comes to flossing since I have such tight gaps between my teeth (which comes from Dad's side of the family, according to her).

Dad was waiting for us at home when Grace and I got back. (Mum couldn't come straight home because she had to go to a meeting again.)

'So how did it go?' he asked us.

'Great!' Grace enthused. 'Mummy says my teeth are perfect, and she let me ride up and down in her chair.'

'Dad, I hate having Mum as our dentist,' I complained. 'Why can't we go somewhere else?'

He ignored that, just as he always does, and asked, 'Where's Bella?'

'Oh, and guess what?' I added swiftly. 'I met Tansy Godwin at the dentist. She says I can text her anytime I want to go round to her place or meet up. Isn't that cool?'

'Tansy Godwin?' His attention was temporarily diverted as he added sharply, 'Michael's daughter?'

'That's right. And guess what? We'll be starting at St Clara's together!'

'Thecla mentioned that was the case.'

'Did she mention anything else … about the Godwins, I mean …?'

Dad scowled. 'Why should she? Libby, where is Bella?'

'Bella? Oh, well …' I decided it was pointless trying to stall for any longer so I told him she'd gone for a walk.

'A walk? Where?'

'Oh, just around the village … She said she wanted to do some thinking.'

'*Thinking?*' Dad made it sound as if the idea of my sister thinking was totally preposterous. 'About *what* exactly?'

Fortunately Grace chose that moment to interrupt. 'Daddy, did you know Aunt Thecla gave me a diamond dog today?'

'It's a diamond brooch,' I explained swiftly to Dad. 'She gave us all diamond brooches. She says they belonged to your mother. They're really valuable.'

'How valuable?' Dad asked with a frown.

'Aunt Thecla says each one is worth five thousand pounds.'

'Our grandpa left them for us when he died,' Grace added.

Dad immediately tensed. 'I think I'd better go and have a word with your aunt once Mum gets home. Where are these brooches now?'

'Still at Aunt Thecla's,' I told him. 'They're really beautiful, Dad.'

'I'm sure they are,' he grunted. 'My mother had very good taste.'

Bella got in an hour later, after failing to answer any of Dad's calls. He was furious with her, and the second she walked into the house he demanded, 'Where have *you* been, young lady?'

My sister shrugged, avoiding his gaze. 'Out.'

'Bella ...' Dad sounded like he was about to ground her for the rest of her life if she didn't give him a proper answer.

'Look, Dad, it's not like *you* tell *us* everything, is it?' she snapped defensively.

'This isn't about me!'

'Actually, it sort of is ...' she persisted defiantly. 'Because you and Mum are our role models, so if *you* don't value the truth, then why should we?'

He gaped at her. So did I. It's at times like these when I honestly think Bella must be more intelligent than she lets on. Or more suicidal.

'Exactly what do you mean by *that*?' Dad growled.

'Well, *you* haven't exactly told *us* the truth about lots of things, have you?'

'*What* things?' he demanded indignantly.

'For starters, you've never told us you were *expelled* from school!'

'What?' I exclaimed loudly.

'It's true! Ask him if you don't believe me!'

I *couldn't* believe it. But I didn't need to ask Dad because I could tell by his face that she wasn't making it up.

'He was sixteen,' Bella went on, 'the same age as Sam when *he* left school! Only unlike Sam – who left because he actually had a job to go to – Dad got kicked out!'

'Who told you all this?' Dad asked her gruffly.

'I just spoke to gossipy Valerie from the uniform shop and she told me. So come on, Dad. What did you *do*?'

'Yes, Dad,' I echoed. 'What *did* you do?'

But whatever Dad had done he clearly didn't think the story was fit for Grace's ears, because he swiftly told Bella and me to stop talking about it in front of her. (Even though she was too engrossed in the TV to bother listening.) 'Come on, Grace. Time to go upstairs. I'll run your bath now.' But before he went he suddenly asked Bella again where she'd been this afternoon. 'I can't believe you spent a whole hour exchanging gossip with Valerie Mayhew.'

As she started to say that she'd gone for a walk because she needed a chance to think, I quickly thought of an excuse that Dad might actually believe.

'She was phoning Sam!' I blurted.

Dad of course had no trouble believing that. He just assumed Sam was still living in our old town. 'I'd rather you phoned him from your bedroom, Bella,' he grunted.

'Why? So you can listen in?' she grunted back.

'Why would I want to listen in?' Dad retorted. 'In fact, I can hardly imagine anything worse! I'd just rather know you were safely up in your room rather than wandering about the streets, that's all. Though you do realise you won't be able to phone Sam every evening once school starts and you've got homework to do.'

'Oh yeah ... because you know all about homework,' Bella said sarcastically. 'Oh no, wait a minute ... I forgot ... you didn't have any homework when you were my age because you'd been *expelled*!'

He just rolled his eyes and headed upstairs to find Grace.

'I can't believe Dad really got expelled!' I said as I joined Bella in the living room. 'What could he have done that was so bad? I mean, this is *Dad* we're talking about!'

'I know! It's great, isn't it?' she said with a grin. 'Every time he has a go at me about school, I am *so* going to throw this back at him!'

'As soon as Grace is in bed I'm going to ask him,' I said.

To be honest I expected the truth was that Dad had been involved in some misguided prank that had gone horribly wrong or that he'd taken the blame for something he hadn't actually done. I was certain he could never have done anything actually *worthy* of expulsion.

But in the end I didn't get the chance to ask him because Mum arrived home just as Dad was putting Grace to bed. Mum immediately took over with Grace, and he told her that he was going round to speak to Aunt Thecla about the brooches.

'Well, if it's your mother's jewellery, surely it's perfectly natural she'd want to pass it on to the girls,' Mum said after he'd explained what had happened. 'Honestly, Paul, I really don't see the problem. In fact, I think it's a very sweet gesture.'

'The problem, Nina, is that any *normal* person would talk it through with us first – not directly hand over fifteen thousand pounds in jewels to three kids. It's ridiculous.'

'Perhaps Aunt Thecla thought you'd say no because it was our grandfather who wanted us to have them,' I suggested.

Mum's mouth twitched at the corners slightly. 'Don't be silly, Libby! I'm sure Daddy isn't that petty.'

Dad grunted that where his father was concerned he *was* that petty. 'I don't want his money,' he murmured. 'Or his valuables.'

'They're not *his* any more – they're Thecla's,' Mum argued. 'Anyway, I thought you'd want the girls to have something that belonged to your mother.'

He seemed really tense when he left the house and I just hoped he and Aunt Thecla weren't about to have an argument. Mum must have been thinking the same thing, because just before he closed the front door she yelled out, 'Whatever she says, Paul, just take a deep breath and count to ten! And remember she's paying the school fees!'

Chapter Sixteen

'I didn't think Dad would actually bring our brooches back with him from Aunt Thecla's. Did you?' I asked Bella as we lay in bed that night.

Bella didn't reply. She was admiring her bird of paradise brooch, which was glittering under the light from the lamp on her bedside table. I knew for Bella it was the brooch itself – the beauty of the thing – that mattered the most, rather than how much it was worth or where it came from.

For me the greatest value lay in the fact that the brooches had once belonged to our grandmother. They were proper family heirlooms that I could imagine my sisters and I passing down to our own daughters one day. I've always wanted to know more about my family, and I love watching programmes on TV where people trace their ancestors and find out more about how they lived and what they were like. I'm really keen to research my family properly one day, though it's going to be hard to get any helpful information out of Dad since he never seems to want to talk about the past.

It turned out that Aunt Thecla had already insured the brooches for us. She said she wanted us to wear them without worrying about them getting lost or stolen. That also meant Dad couldn't complain about the cost of having to insure them himself. Mum and Dad had still got Grace and me to hand ours over to them for safe-keeping, but Bella had refused, saying she was old enough to look after her brooch herself.

'I bet Sam's glad he's not sleeping outside tonight,' I whispered. The rain was clattering down outside and I wondered how the cottage roof was holding up and whether Sam had enough containers to place under all the leaks.

Bella just grunted and reached out to turn off the light.

'So why do you think Dad got expelled from school?' I whispered into the semi-darkness.

'Who cares?' she muttered.

'But don't you think it's really weird that we never heard about it before?'

131

'It's not that big a deal, Libby. Now shut up. I'm going to sleep.'

'But I was only saying –'

'Well, *don't*!' She pulled the covers over her head, grumbling about what a pain it was having to share a room with me.

I suddenly thought of something. 'Bella, is your period due?' Mum always seems to know when Bella's period is due just by how moody she's being. Mum says all those extra hormones don't only give you spots and greasy hair – they can also give you a really bad temper.

Unfortunately, instead of appreciating my insight Bella made a strangled noise like a wild animal being physically restrained from killing someone. 'Just because I don't want to answer your dumb questions, Libby, it doesn't mean I'm *pre-menstrual*!' she yelled. 'God, you're even worse than Mum!'

I decided not to risk talking to her again after that.

The following morning I woke to hear arguing coming from downstairs. It sounded like Mum and Bella were having a massive row. I had a shower and quickly went back into our bedroom to get dressed. By the time I went downstairs, Dad was in the bathroom and Mum and Grace had gone out. Grace had been complaining that Mum never spends any time with her since we moved, and even though that's not true, Mum had felt so guilty she'd promised to devote the whole of her day off to a Grace-and-Mummy expedition. I have to admit I felt a bit cross about the way she could wrap Mum around her little finger like that. I mean, I can't even remember the last time Mum and I did anything special together and you don't see me making all that fuss about it.

Bella was lying on the sofa, still in her pyjamas, a hot-water bottle pressed against her belly. She looked cross. As soon as she saw me she snapped, 'Don't *you* start!' even though I hadn't so much as opened my mouth.

'Why were you and Mum yelling?' I asked.

'She took away my phone! She was yacking on and asking me stuff while I was trying to text, and then she got all huffy cos I wasn't listening, so she grabbed it off me. Says I should be "resting" until the cramps stop.'

'I expect she's just trying to help,' I ventured tentatively.

'What do *you* know about it?' she snapped.

I left her lying there watching TV and went into the kitchen to fix myself breakfast.

Bella has always suffered with period pain, though it's

been a lot better since she got some stronger painkillers from the doctor. I have to say that the prospect of starting my own periods scares me a bit, even though Mum says most girls don't have as much of a problem as Bella. Some of the girls in my class had started by the end of Year Seven, and Mum says she doesn't think it will be long before mine start too. Whoopee – *not*!

The doorbell rang just as I was pouring milk on to my cereal. Since Dad was still in the bathroom – probably sitting on the loo reading a newspaper with no intention of emerging anytime soon – I put down my cereal bowl with a bit of a thud and went to see who was there.

I opened the front door to find nobody. Sticking my head out to have a proper look I heard a whistle to my left, and when I looked down the road a bit further I could see Sam standing there. I quickly put the door on the latch and ran down the road to meet him. Close up I thought his face seemed thinner than usual and he had dark circles under his eyes.

'What are you doing here?' I asked him.

'I need to speak to Bella. She hasn't answered the texts just sent.'

'Mum took away her phone. She isn't dressed yet. She's not feeling very well.'

His immediate look of concern was quite sweet. 'What's wrong with her?'

'She … umm … well, she's got her … you know …' I had difficulty telling him without blushing.

Fortunately Sam seemed to get my meaning. 'Oh right …' he murmured. I doubted Bella talked about her periods much to him, but then again, I had no idea what sort of stuff almost-sixteen-year-old girls talked to their seventeen-year-old boyfriends about. I can't even imagine *having* a boyfriend myself, though I've had a few fantasy versions over the last couple of years (one of them is an actor in a TV show I really like, and another is the seriously cute drummer in my favourite boy band).

'OK, well, I came to tell her I have a job – at least for a couple of weeks. The bloke at the garage down the road needs somebody to help him while his apprentice is off sick.'

I immediately perked up. 'Oh, Sam, that's great.'

'Yeah, it doesn't pay loads but it's enough to go back to the B & B if I want. It's OK at the cottage for now, so I'll save my money and stay on there until the neighbours come back.'

'So long as you're careful not to get caught,' I said, because I still wasn't very happy about the risk he was taking. 'Bella will be really pleased when I tell her about the job,' I added. 'Well done, Sam.'

He grinned. 'Thank you, Libby. Tell Bella to text me when she gets her phone back.' He left with a cheery wave.

For the next few days nothing much happened. Mum was at work a lot, Dad worked on his computer at home and Grace spent a lot of time drawing and painting at Aunt Thecla's house.

But then one morning when Bella and I were home alone (Dad was out meeting a new client) the phone started ringing.

I picked up to hear Aunt Thecla's voice at the other end sounding distraught. 'Libby? Has Grace come home?'

'No. Why? Isn't she with you?'

'She was but we've had an argument. I can't find her, and I'm not sure if she's hiding in the house somewhere or if she's gone outside.'

'She knows she's not allowed outside on her own. She's probably hiding. Do you want us to come over and help you look?'

'That might be a good idea. If she hears you she might come out.'

I started to ask what it was they'd argued about, but she promptly hung up.

In Aunt Thecla's kitchen there was evidence of Grace's recent art lesson. Pastel crayons and sheets of paper were still lying on the table and the new art smock our aunt had bought for her was lying abandoned on top of a stool.

'So what did you row about?' Bella asked immediately.

Aunt Thecla turned and picked up a tin from the work surface behind her. 'This! Fifty pounds is missing from my money tin.'

I instantly felt queasy. Despite my nagging, Bella still hadn't replaced the money she'd taken. I looked at her to see what she would say.

Bella looked decidedly uncomfortable but I don't think Aunt Thecla noticed. Our aunt isn't always good at reading people's body language or guessing how they're feeling. Most of the time that makes life more difficult but just occasionally it can come in handy.

'Are you sure?' Bella asked, carefully avoiding any eye contact with either me or our aunt.

'Of course I'm sure. I took the tin down this morning to check it. There's only half the amount that there should be! Grace is the only one who's been in my kitchen recently, so I asked her if she'd taken it. She said no, so I said I would be checking her pockets and asking your parents to search her room at home, so she had better own up at once if she was lying. And that's when she burst into tears and started throwing crayons on the floor. I never knew she had such a temper!'

'Well, you shouldn't have accused her of stealing!' I snapped before I could stop myself. 'No wonder she's upset!'

'Grace would never steal anything!' Bella chipped in, just as hotly.

But instead of backing down Aunt Thecla promptly reminded us of the time a couple of years back when she'd gone to the supermarket at Christmastime with Grace, who had managed to hide a little gold-foiled chocolate teddy bear in her pocket without being spotted. Aunt Thecla hadn't discovered it until she got home and had been far too mortified to take it back, and by the time Dad got home Mum had already let Grace eat it. (In fact, Mum seemed to view Grace's shoplifting episode as some sort of major achievement, worthy of recounting as a funny story for ages afterwards to all our friends and family.)

'She was only four then and it's not the same,' I protested. 'It's not like she's ever stolen anything since.'

'Well, someone must have taken my money,' Aunt Thecla persisted crossly. 'And since Grace is the one who's been here the most I thought it a reasonable assumption. Anyway … I merely asked her. I didn't accuse her.'

'You threatened to search her room!' I scoffed. 'You're basically talking about frisking her before she leaves! Of course you're accusing her, Aunt Thecla!'

I turned to Bella, expecting her to agree with me, but to my annoyance she'd left the kitchen. I could hear her on the stairs calling out Grace's name.

Just as I was considering telling Aunt Thecla the truth – or at least a version of it that would prove Grace's innocence – Bella yelled down, 'I think she's in your art room, Aunt Thecla! The door's open!'

'*What?* She knows she's not allowed in there!' She set off up the two flights of stairs to the top of the house at a much faster pace than usual.

'I think you must have left the key in the lock,' Bella said as we caught her up outside the attic room. 'I've just looked inside and she's definitely there.' For some reason she was grinning slyly. 'Cool paintings, Aunt Thecla.'

'Wait here,' she snapped.

But we both ignored that instruction and followed her into the room. I was really curious to see inside for the first time.

Straight away we found Grace curled up under a table against the wall, a massive pout on her face. On top of the table were various paint pots and jars of dirty water with brushes in them, plus a couple of half-empty mugs of tea and some rough unfinished paintings. 'Grace!' Aunt Thecla scolded her at once. 'You know you're not allowed in here. I hope you haven't touched any of my work.'

'If you can call it work,' Bella whispered in my ear. 'I mean, just because you've got an art studio in your house it doesn't make you a professional artist, does it?'

I didn't reply. To be fair, I don't remember Aunt Thecla ever referring to herself as a professional, although I suppose the way she acts tends to give that impression. For instance she calls any time she spends in her attic studio 'working', and she talks as if it's only a matter of time before she starts to sell her paintings.

'Oh wow! It's Hughie!' I exclaimed as I took in the half-finished painting on an easel by the window. There was a photograph of him clipped to the top-left corner of the paper. I could already tell it was going to be one of her better pieces.

My gaze drifted around the walls on which were displayed lots of Aunt Thecla's work. There were several paintings done in some weird abstract style on one wall and on another there was nothing but paintings and sketches of nudes. They were actually very good – if a bit embarrassing to view with my aunt watching.

'I did those at an art class a long time ago,' she said, seeing me staring at them.

'Oh yeah? What about that one?' Bella asked, pointing with a grin at a much larger painting of a young man standing in a field of bluebells. It was by far the best painting in the room and the only one in a frame. The subject of the picture wore only a red sarong tied around his waist and stood with his back to the artist. His upper body was tanned and muscular and he had curly shoulder-length blond hair.

'Is that a sexy back or what?' Bella commented cheekily. 'So was he your boyfriend, Aunt Thecla?'

She hesitated for just a moment too long before saying, 'Don't be ridiculous, Bella.'

I looked again at the picture, taking in the blond curly hair, the slim muscular body. Wait a minute … Surely this couldn't be …?

Aunt Thecla's face was pink and she looked away from us as she added, 'Now, out of here, all of you. Grace – that includes you! Get out from under that table AT ONCE!'

Grace jumped when our aunt shouted and in her scramble to escape she banged her head on the table, sending a jam jar full of dirty water and brushes crashing on to the floor.

'Get OUT!' Aunt Thecla screamed at us, and as she rushed to rescue everything we raced downstairs and out through the front door as fast as we could.

Chapter Seventeen

As soon as we got home Grace started to whine about how she wanted Mum. Sometimes if she's really upset Mum will have a quick chat with her on the phone in between patients, but neither Bella nor I wanted to ring Mum until we'd had a bit more time to think about what to say. The last thing we wanted was for the truth to come out about Aunt Thecla's missing money.

'I don't think we should distract Mummy at work, Grace,' I pointed out.

'She won't mind,' Grace said stubbornly.

'She will if she pulls out the wrong tooth!' Bella snapped.

Suddenly we heard the front door opening. It was Dad. Bella and I looked at each other in alarm. His meeting must have finished early.

'Daddy!' Grace squealed, rushing up to him and

flinging herself into his arms. 'Daddy, Aunt Thecla was really mean to me!' And she burst into tears.

Unfortunately Dad always responds well to a show of fierce clinging and shirt-dampening tears from Grace. 'Why? What did she do?' he asked at once.

Grace's crying was preventing her from answering straight away, but Bella and I both knew we only had a few minutes before she told him everything.

'Let's get her a drink of water, Libby,' Bella said, quickly pulling me after her into the kitchen and shutting the door behind us.

It was time to decide what our story was going to be.

'We've only got two options,' I whispered. 'You either confess you took the money, or we pretend we know nothing about it. If you confess, Mum and Dad are going to be furious and they'll want to know why. But if we keep quiet then Grace will still be a suspect, which isn't really fair.'

'It can't *only* be Grace who's had the opportunity to take it,' Bella said with a cross frown. 'Hasn't Aunt Thecla got a cleaning lady or somebody like that?'

'Bella, it's lucky she *doesn't*!' I snapped. 'Can you imagine if her cleaning lady got fired because of us? We'd *have* to own up then!'

144

'Not necessarily,' she said stubbornly. 'After all, it's not *our* fault if Aunt Thecla goes around accusing innocent people instead of finding out the truth first.'

I glared at her. Sometimes I just can't believe how pig-headed my sister can be. Or how selfish. 'Bella, Aunt Thecla's just given us that really expensive jewellery, *and* she's paying for our new school and ... and ... you *stole* from her! How can you blame *her* for any of this?'

She was looking a bit taken aback by my sharp words, then Dad shouted to us from the other room. 'Bella! Libby! Come in here!'

'I think we should tell the truth,' I said. 'Just that you borrowed the money. Not about Sam!'

'No,' Bella said in a panicky voice. 'They'll want to know *why* I took it. They might even guess it's to do with Sam. Libby, we *can't* tell them.' She gave me her most desperate pleading look.

'GIRLS!' Dad sounded impatient and his voice was nearer.

'OK!' I caved, just as he flung open the kitchen door to glare at us.

But it wasn't us that Dad was really angry with. It was Aunt Thecla. After we confirmed Grace's version of what happened at our aunt's house, he snarled, 'That's it! I'm *not* having her accuse Grace like that! From now on, you three don't go near your aunt without me or Mum with you! Do you understand? Libby and Bella, stay here with your sister until I get back.'

'Where are you going?' I called after him as he headed for the door.

But he didn't reply.

'So what do we do now?' I asked miserably as the front door slammed behind him and Grace burst into tears again.

'You stay here and babysit,' Bella grunted. 'I'm going out.'

'Wait ... we'll come with you ...'

'No. I don't want you two tagging along.' And two seconds later she was gone.

I guessed she must be going to see Sam. Since he'd started working at the local garage she'd been popping in to see him on his lunch breaks. I didn't want to be stuck inside on my own with Grace so I offered to take her to the park on her scooter. 'Let's have a look at Dad and Aunt Thecla's old house on the way there. Tansy lives right next to it, so we can see if she wants to come to the park too. I'll just send her a text to tell her we're on our way.'

* * *

146

Ten minutes later I was shouting for Grace to slow down as she scooted along on the pavement ahead of me. 'This is the street,' I yelled out. 'Start looking for the right number.'

Each house stood on its own, set back from the road along a short drive. Most of them had large front gardens with high gates at the entrance. We'd driven past Dad's old house a couple of times before but he'd never wanted to stop and have a proper look.

'This is it,' I told Grace as we reached a grey sandstone house set in a large garden, which we couldn't see properly because it was surrounded by a high brick wall.

'I wonder which bedroom was Daddy's,' Grace said, looking in through the impressive black wrought-iron gates that guarded the entrance.

'I don't know,' I said. 'You should ask him.'

We stood at the gates for a while staring in at the house where Dad had spent his childhood. Somehow it was really hard to imagine him ever belonging here.

'Let's see if Tansy's in,' I said, turning my attention to the house next door. Tansy hadn't answered my text message but that didn't mean we couldn't call on her.

'Look, it's for sale,' Grace pointed out excitedly. 'Maybe we can buy it!'

Sure enough, there was an estate agent's board nailed to the gatepost of the neighbouring house.

'Somehow I don't think Mum and Dad could afford any of the houses in this road,' I murmured as I stared at the house through its open gates.

That's when we saw Tansy waving to us from one of the downstairs bay windows.

'Let's go and see her!' Grace said.

'Wait for me,' I called, but she was already bolting ahead of me up the gravel drive towards the house.

Chapter Eighteen

Tansy opened the large front door and shouted a greeting as I followed my sister up the drive.

Grace immediately started chatting away to Tansy on the doorstep, while behind them I could see a big gloomy hall and dark furniture.

'We're on our way to the park,' I explained. 'Did you get my text?'

'Just saw it. That park up the road is pretty rubbish.'

'We can visit you instead if you like,' Grace offered eagerly.

She grinned. 'Sure. Come on in.'

Grace dived straight past her and rushed over to an old-fashioned rocking horse, which she'd obviously had her eye on. She immediately began to pet it like it was real.

I followed her into the hall. 'Are you on your own?' I asked, since the house seemed quiet apart from us.

'Yeah. Dad's off to see his lawyer and then the estate agent. He won't be back for ages.' She closed the heavy front door with a bang.

'I thought you were moving in – not selling,' I said.

'Dad wants to buy somewhere smaller. And less gloomy, he says!'

'Why *is* your house so gloomy?' Grace asked.

Tansy grinned. 'Grandpa used to say that the ghosts liked it that way.'

'Ghosts?' Grace looked half-scared and half-thrilled.

'Ghosts aren't real, Grace,' I told her quickly.

'Some people believe in them though,' Tansy said. 'My grandpa did, sort of, but then he got pretty weird when he got old. He used to tell me stories about the ghost of my uncle who I'm supposed to take after. There are lots of pictures of him in the front room. Come on, I'll show you.'

Grace suddenly announced, 'My friend actually saw a *real* ghost without a head.'

'Really? That's cool.' Tansy was smiling. 'Was it carrying its head under its arm? I hear a lot of ghosts do that.'

'No – it had lots of blood running down its neck where its head had been chopped off. It was in a big palace that belonged to Henry of the Eighth.'

'Wow! So do you think the ghost was one of his wives?'

Grace nodded. 'It definitely was! And Bella says it had to be his number two or number five wife because they were the only ones who got their heads chopped off.' She started chanting the rhyme Bella had taught her: 'Divorced, beheaded, died … divorced, beheaded, survived …' over and over again until I told her to shut up.

Tansy led us into a large old-fashioned room and stopped in front of a painting of a boy in his late teens dressed in hunting clothes. He had blond hair and a freckled face with laughing blue eyes and he closely resembled Tansy.

'This is my uncle Murray Godwin,' she said. 'He was my dad's older brother. He died when he was twenty.'

As I glanced around the room I saw there were lots of photos in frames displayed everywhere, and many of them seemed to be of the same boy. Tansy had become really animated as she showed me them and I realised this was something we had in common – we were both interested in old photos. Maybe I'd finally found someone with whom I could share my enthusiasm about the past.

'Grandpa hasn't changed much in this room since my grandma died,' Tansy told us. 'She died twelve years ago – a few days after I was born. Grandpa said she would have died sooner but she was hanging on so she could meet me. Apparently I was the exact likeness of Uncle Murray when *he* was born, so my grandma was really pleased.' She joined me by the mantelpiece, where I was looking at more photos of the same young boy. 'They're all him,' she said. 'Him as a baby, him as a little boy, him as a scout, him and my dad at St Quentin's – that's the stupid school that expelled your dad –'

'Wait, you *know* about my dad being expelled?'

Before Tansy could respond, Grace interrupted us. 'I'm bored! Can I go in the garden?'

'Sure,' Tansy said. 'I'll come and open the back door.'

While they were gone I spotted a photograph of four children – three boys and one girl. The smallest boy was definitely Dad but I didn't recognise the others. The girl had a mass of dark wavy hair – very similar to mine except it was a lot longer – and I suddenly realised who she was. 'Aunt Thecla,' I murmured, struggling to match the girl's eyes, full of mischief and excitement, with the stern glinty eyes of the woman I knew today. Perhaps there was a certain determination in her gaze, which remained the same, but it was difficult to see much of a likeness.

I stared at the photograph for ages. It felt so strange to see Dad and Aunt Thecla in someone else's photograph in someone else's house. The other two boys in the picture had blond hair – the older boy's was clipped short while the younger's was shaggy and curly. The younger boy had his arm around the girl.

As Tansy walked back into the room she said, 'That was taken on Murray's twelfth birthday. The cricket bat he's holding was his birthday present. He was really good at batting and Grandpa thought he was good enough to play professional cricket, so he bought him this top-quality super-expensive bat. But Murray didn't want to be a cricketer. All he cared about was travelling.'

'Is that your dad?' I pointed to the young boy with his arm around Aunt Thecla – the one with the curly hair.

Tansy nodded. 'My dad and your aunt were the same age and they were best friends. They started dating when they were fifteen.' She grinned. 'Apparently *your* dad got really jealous and protective because he worshipped his big sister.'

I was surprised. 'Really?'

'Yes. My dad used to take your aunt on secret picnics in the countryside. She always had a sketchpad with her and sometimes she'd draw him. Dad was pretty handsome when he was young.' She sounded proud.

'Did your dad still have curly hair when he grew up?'

'Yeah – until he left university. Then he started getting buzz cuts. Why?'

'It's just, I think I might have seen an actual painting Aunt Thecla did of him.'

'Really? I'd *love* to see it.'

'And I'd love to show you.' I started to rack my brain to think of a way. I wasn't sure if it was going to be that easy to sneak her into Aunt Thecla's art studio. 'Leave it to me,' I said.

'You know, it's weird,' Tansy said as she glanced at the photograph of the four children. 'You look at them there and you can hardly believe what happened to them all …'

'What *did* happen?' I asked curiously.

'Well …' She pointed to each child in turn, starting with her uncle. 'First Murray died in an accident in India, then my dad and your aunt broke off their engagement, and then your dad got caught breaking and entering and got sent away for two years.'

'Excuse me?' I just about choked on this last piece of information.

'Your dad must have told you?' She started to look uncomfortable as I stood gaping at her. 'OK, so maybe he

154

hasn't told you … maybe you should just forget *I* told you …'

I shook my head. 'Tell me *everything*,' I said as I plonked myself down on the nearest seat to let her know I wasn't going anywhere until she did.

So Tansy sat down on the sofa beside me and told me what she knew. Most of the story had come directly from her dad and I felt a little envious of how much he'd shared with her. Tansy clearly knew loads about her family and about her dad's childhood. It was so different to how private my own dad was on the subject.

'Your dad was sixteen at the time,' she began. 'Your aunt and *my* dad were eighteen and they were engaged. On the day it happened my grandparents were taking my uncle Murray to the airport because he was leaving to go travelling. My dad didn't go with them because he was studying for his A levels … Anyway, after a couple of hours he got fed up and went out for a bit of a break. When he got back he found his parents arriving home much earlier than he'd expected. And my grandpa had just caught your dad inside their house. He'd broken in to steal Murray's cricket bat!'

'No way!' I couldn't believe Dad would ever break

155

into someone else's house, let alone steal anything. And I instantly felt as if I liked Tansy a bit less for telling the story, even though I know you're not supposed to blame the messenger.

'It's true!' Tansy insisted. 'My grandpa agreed not to call the police, but he told the school and that's why they expelled him. Your dad got sent away to a really strict boarding school for delinquent boys.'

'That can't be right!' I exclaimed in disbelief, because I'd never heard any of this before. Then again, Dad had only just admitted that he'd been expelled from school – and so far he hadn't told us anything about the reason why.

'Bluebell – I mean your aunt – broke off her engagement to my dad after that,' Tansy added. 'He was devastated because he really loved her.'

'Wait, are you saying Aunt Thecla was the one who broke it off? Are you sure?' I'd always understood it to be the other way round. In fact, I was pretty certain that Dad also believed it was Aunt Thecla who'd been jilted.

'Definitely. My dad says that in retrospect he doesn't think he ever got over it, even after he married my mum. Which is probably why their marriage didn't last very long.'

'Your dad really told you all that?'

She nodded. 'He talks to me about everything.'

I frowned, trying to imagine my own father confiding in me to that extent.

Suddenly my phone started ringing. It was Dad, sounding cross and wanting to know where the three of us were.

'Grace is with me. We're at Tansy's house.' It felt weird to be talking to my here-and-now dad after hearing what Tansy had just revealed about him.

There was a brief silence. 'Come home now please. And ring Bella. I've tried her phone but she's not taking my calls.'

'Trouble?' Tansy asked when I hung up.

'Not really. Just … well … I'd better get Grace.' But before I left the room I found my gaze lingering for just a few seconds longer on the photo of those four smiling children from the past.

Chapter Nineteen

'Bella, what are we going to do now?' I asked her the second I woke up the following morning.

'About what?' she grunted as she turned her back on me to finish getting dressed. Mum was taking her shopping for new clothes in Castle Westbury which was the only reason she was up this early.

'You *know* what!' I snapped. Sometimes I really feel like I could throttle her.

The day before, Dad and Aunt Thecla had had a massive row. At first Mum was on Dad's side when she heard how our aunt had accused Grace of stealing. But when she heard Dad's account of the confrontation he'd had with Aunt Thecla, she started to get angry with him instead.

'You do realise we're depending on her for the school fees, don't you, Paul? Couldn't you have tempered what you said just a little?'

'I'm not going to let her bully our children,' Dad said crossly.

'That's all very well but we can't afford to pay three lots of school fees if you completely fall out with her,' Mum said sharply.

'Nina, she's already put money in a trust to pay the fees. She told me yesterday that just before he died our father said he wanted her to use some of his money to benefit the girls. Can you believe that? So apparently the school fees will get paid no matter what.'

'Really?' Mum sounded relieved. 'But we're still indebted to her, Paul. I'm going round there to try and clear this up. Perhaps if I sit down with her and talk things through, she'll think of someone other than Grace who's had the opportunity to take her money.'

I shot a worried glance at Bella when I heard that, but she wasn't looking at me.

Dad said, 'I'll tell you what I think happened. She took the money herself and then forgot about it. It's easily done. I told her that's what probably happened, but of course Thecla takes that as a huge insult. Apparently the idea that her memory might have let her down is far less palatable than the idea that Gracie stole her precious fifty quid.'

'Paul, would you stop talking like that –'

I pulled Bella away while they were still discussing it. I was already sure that the best way to stop this from escalating was for the missing money to turn up – and fast.

'Bella, we have to put that money back,' I whispered.

'We haven't *got* it to put back!' she protested.

'Well, Sam has a job now, so –'

'No way,' Bella interrupted me fiercely. 'He's not getting paid much, and there's no way Aunt Thecla needs that money more than him.'

And she stubbornly refused to listen to anything else I had to say on the subject.

There was something else I'd been thinking about a lot, which was the conversation I'd had with Tansy. I really wanted to talk to Dad about it. In fact, the more I thought about how angry he was with Aunt Thecla for accusing Grace of stealing, the more I wondered about the story Tansy had told me. Could that be the reason Dad was so angry? Because he knew how it felt to be wrongly accused? Because I was absolutely certain that Dad hadn't stolen Murray's cricket bat or anything else when he was sixteen, no matter how bad things had looked.

I made sure Grace was out of earshot before I brought up the subject with Dad after Mum and Bella had gone out.

'Dad, you know when I went round to Tansy's house yesterday ...' I began, as I sat beside him at the table.

'Yes?' He'd just settled down to drink a mug of coffee while flicking through the newspaper and he looked a bit annoyed by the interruption.

I took a deep breath, deciding to get straight to the point. 'Well, Tansy told me why you got expelled from school.'

He put his paper down and looked at me. 'Oh yes. And what did she tell you?'

I swallowed and said in a rush, 'Her grandfather caught you stealing from his house.'

He kept looking at me and I felt really tense. 'And do you think that's true?' he finally asked.

'No,' I said at once. 'I think he caught you in his house and *thought* you were stealing.'

Dad took a big swig of coffee. 'I guess you want to know the whole story?'

I nodded, but just then Grace came running into the room. 'When are we leaving, Daddy?' she asked. Apparently he'd promised to take her out for a bike ride.

'Soon, sweetheart. Tell you what, you go upstairs and get ready. Make sure you brush your teeth really well or Mummy will get cross.'

As she raced off to do as he'd asked, he turned back to me and said quietly, 'I don't mind telling you, but I'm not sure there's time right now.'

'There's time. *Please*, Dad,' I begged him.

So he told me what had happened when he was sixteen.

'It was the day Michael's older brother, Murray, was flying off to India. His parents were driving him to the airport, and after they left Thecla told me she was going round to see Michael. She wasn't meant to be seeing him that day because he had an exam to study for, so she asked me to cover for her if our dad noticed she was gone.

'Michael's parents came back earlier than expected. Apparently they'd argued with Murray and hadn't stayed at the airport to have a meal with him as they'd planned. They stopped off at our house to talk to my father about Thecla and Michael's engagement. They didn't approve of it and they wanted the wedding postponed for as long as possible. Well, anyway ... I was worried about Thecla getting caught next door so I went to warn her.

'No one came to the front door when I rang the bell

so I decided to sneak in through the French windows at the back. I knew those patio doors didn't lock properly because Murray used to sneak in that way sometimes if he was late home. The house was very quiet when I got inside, so I thought the two of them were probably upstairs in Michael's bedroom …'

'Rolling about on the bed together, snogging?' I suggested with a giggle.

He winced. 'Something like that. Anyway, I knew I had to go and warn them – however embarrassing it was – so I headed for the stairs. On my way through the hall I spotted the cricket bat Murray had promised to give me before he left. He must have forgotten about it in all the rush. I thought I may as well claim it while I was there, so I picked it up. Just then the front door opened and Mr and Mrs Godwin walked in.'

'DADDY!' came my little sister's voice from upstairs. 'I NEED YOU!'

I quickly put my arm on Dad's to keep him from going. 'Leave her, Dad. She's old enough to wipe her own bum! So what happened next?'

'Michael suddenly appeared from the kitchen and made it pretty clear he knew nothing about me being there – or about Murray giving the bat to me. He looked pretty flustered so I guessed he must have been smuggling Thecla out through the kitchen door just as I was sneaking in through the French windows.'

I frowned. 'But I don't think Aunt Thecla was –'

'DADDY I CAN'T REACH THE TOILET PAPER!' Grace yelled.

Dad stood up, talking rapidly as he headed for the stairs. 'Mr Godwin was furious, needless to say! He called my father, who persuaded him not to call the police and promised to punish me when he got me home. But Mr Godwin decided that wasn't enough. He was a governor at my school and he knew my headmaster very well. Suffice it to say, he had a lot of influence in those days and he managed to get me expelled.'

'Dad ... that's ... that's ...' I didn't know what to say, but he had already gone upstairs to sort out Grace.

When he came down again I was still sitting at the table. I was thinking how Tansy's version of the story hadn't included the part about Thecla being in the house with Michael that day. So much for Tansy's dad telling her *everything*, I thought. 'It's not fair though,' I said as he sat down with me again. 'Aunt Thecla should have told them the *real* reason you went there! It's not like you broke in just to steal that bat.'

164

'She said she was afraid for Michael if his father found out he'd been with her all afternoon instead of studying for whatever A level he had the following day.'

'She should still have tried to help you more,' I insisted. 'After all, you wouldn't have got into so much trouble if you hadn't been trying to help *her*.'

'And myself, remember – to Murray's cricket bat!' he said with a little grin. 'I was far from blameless, Libby. Though he honestly *had* told me I could have it. It just seemed like he'd forgotten to mention it to anyone else!'

'Hey, is this the thing you haven't forgiven Aunt Thecla for?' I was remembering the bits of conversation I'd overheard between him and Mum. 'Because it was really *her* fault you got caught inside Mr Godwin's house and she didn't stand up for you afterwards!'

Dad gave me a strange sort of look then, almost as if he was fighting back some unexpected emotion that he didn't want me to see. 'You know, this may seem hard to believe but I was completely devoted to Thecla back then. I suppose, what with losing our mother when we were still young ... I think I'd have done anything for her. Anyway, she said she hadn't *asked* me to go inside the Godwins' house to try and find her – and that she certainly hadn't asked me to take that blasted bat! She said I had

165

made my own bed so I would just have to lie in it!' He gave a weary smile. 'I guess she had a point, but ...'

'It hurt?' I suggested.

He nodded.

I felt frustrated. 'Listen, I know it was the dark ages and that you didn't have mobiles and the internet and stuff ... but Murray must have phoned home from India at *some* point. Couldn't they have asked *him* about the bat?'

'Ah well ...' Dad swallowed. 'It was only a couple of weeks later that we got the news that he'd been killed in an accident.'

'Oh ...' I'd momentarily forgotten that part of the story.

Dad looked sad as he continued. 'He was the other person I'd really looked up to as a boy. I guess I just ... well, I stopped looking up to anyone and gave up seeing the point in anything for a while. It was an awful time ... I was actually quite glad to be sent away ...'

'To boarding school?' I murmured softly.

He nodded. 'My father found a boarding school that was meant to be good at handling academically able boys with difficult behaviour. He threatened to disown me if I got myself expelled from there before I'd completed my A levels.'

'Oh, and he *did* disown you, didn't he?' I said. 'So was *that* why?'

Dad shook his head. 'The school was very strict – most of the boys who went there needed very firm boundaries. But it was a small school and the headmaster took a great interest in all of us, and the teachers were decent enough so long as you toed the line. I behaved myself and worked hard and got good A levels. My father was pleased with me for once. He valued education very highly, you see.' He sighed. 'The big row came when I told him I didn't intend to go to university like he wanted.' He sighed again. 'You know, it must be so easy for kids who actually *want* the same things that their parents want for them.

'Anyway, when I refused to take up my place at Oxford, my father couldn't deal with it. He made it perfectly clear I was a massive disappointment to him. He said he was ashamed to call me his son. Well, I guess *I* couldn't deal with *that* … I told him I didn't have to do what he said and that I didn't need his money. He challenged me to see how I got on without it. That's when he disowned me. We became completely estranged and we never spoke again! It's something I suppose I should regret – and sometimes I do – but the truth is I'm sure the rest of my life has been a lot easier without him

breathing down my neck and criticising everything I do.'
He looked at me almost apologetically. 'But I don't mean
to burden *you* with all this stuff from the past, Libby.
You've got your own life to live.'

'It's OK, Dad. I like hearing about the past,' I said,
feeling like I understood him so much better from this
one conversation. And I have to say I also felt pretty
proud that he was sharing all this with me.

Chapter Twenty

I don't know why but there was something about Dad's story that made me want to take action. I wanted to do what *I* knew was right instead of always listening to Bella.

So I decided to go and talk to Sam.

I waited for Dad and Grace to leave, then I set off to find Sam at the garage. I deliberately didn't text him to say I was coming because I didn't want him texting Bella to find out why. I knew she would try and stop me from speaking to him if she could.

Before I left I went up to my bedroom to brush my hair, and while I was there I spotted Bella's make-up bag on her bed. *A bit of mascara and eyeliner might make me look older, which might make Sam take me more seriously*, I thought. I briefly considered using Bella's eyelash curlers as well but decided against it. I'd tried them before and pinched my eyelid painfully in the process, plus I really didn't want to risk making my eyelashes look too clumpy.

I don't often wear make-up and I was quite pleased with the result.

I arrived at the village garage to find Sam on the fore-court helping a stoutish grey-haired man, who I presumed was the owner.

'Hi, Sam,' I greeted him.

He looked up, clearly surprised to see me. 'Hi, Libby. Is everything OK?'

'Yes. But listen, I need to speak to you really urgently about something. Have you got a minute?'

Sam looked a bit worried as he asked his boss if it was OK to take a quick break.

'Take your tea break now, if you like. You can bring me back a brew from the caff. Tell them I'll pay at lunchtime.'

'Sure, Bill.' Sam turned back to me. 'Come on then.'

As he led me to the greasy spoon across the road I couldn't help thinking that it wasn't every day I got taken out to a café by a cute older boy. I sat down at a table – away from the window in case anyone we knew happened to pass by – while Sam went over to the counter to buy himself a drink. I couldn't help wondering if any of the other people in the café actually thought he was my boyfriend.

'You need building up,' I told him as he came over to the table. He was quite a lot thinner than usual, despite the food my sister had been stealing for him.

He grinned. 'You sound like Bella.'

'Well, it's true.' I started to worry then about whether I was doing the right thing asking him to return the £50 out of his wages. I didn't want to leave him without enough money for food.

'Your mum must be really worried about you,' I said, stalling for time.

'I've texted her. She knows I'm OK. Now what's this about?'

'Well ... Bella doesn't want me to tell you this but ...' I blurted out how she had taken Aunt Thecla's money to give to him, and how Grace had been accused of stealing it. And how we really needed to put the money back as soon as possible.

I have to admit that I hadn't expected him to look so mortified when I told him about the stolen money. And I certainly hadn't expected him to get so angry with Bella. 'She never told me that money was your aunt's!'

'She was only doing it to help you,' I said.

'I don't want that sort of help!' He reached inside his jeans pocket and took out a battered wallet. 'Here.' He took out two twenty-pound notes and gave them to me. 'I'll borrow the rest from Bill. He'll be paying me again tomorrow anyhow.' His cheeks were flushed and even the tips of his ears had gone pink. Clearly this was a really big deal for him.

'What are you doing?' I asked nervously as he started texting.

'Telling Bella to meet me here later.'

'Sam, she didn't mean –' I began, but before I could finish he was standing up, leaving his drink on the table and making an angry exit.

I followed him out. 'Sam!' I called, running to catch him up, but he ignored me as he strode across the road to the garage.

His boss was inside the workshop, eating a banana. 'So where's my tea?' he asked.

'Oh … sorry … I'll go back and get it … but, Bill … I owe Libby here some money. Would it be OK if I got ten pound from my wages today?'

Bill sighed. 'Wait here.'

'Sorry,' I whispered to Sam as we waited in silence for Bill to return.

'It's not your fault,' he grunted.

Bill came back and handed him two ten-pound notes, shaking his head as Sam tried to give one of them back. 'You'll need some cash for yourself. Now get back to work. I'll fetch my own tea.'

I hurried home wondering when I would get the chance to plant the fifty pounds back in our aunt's kitchen. I would have to be careful not to make it too obvious. If she found the money just after I'd visited she would know who had put it there.

I checked my watch, trying to work out when Bella and Mum would be back from their shopping trip to Castle Westbury. They'd gone by bus and intended to go somewhere for lunch so I guessed they would be a while. Dad and Grace were hopefully still cycling.

I wondered if Bella had seen Sam's message yet and whether she'd texted him back. I was really dreading her reaction when she found out what I'd done.

I got home to find Tansy waiting outside our front door, holding her phone. When she saw me she swiftly put it away. 'There you are! I was just going to send you a text. I've got some really BIG news! You're never going to believe this but ... my dad has just gone out for lunch with your aunt!'

'*What?*'

'Dad says they're meeting up purely as friends, but then he always says that whenever he asks someone out on a date.'

'A *date*? Are you *serious*?'

'Absolutely. You know, I think my mum's right. I think Dad *is* still carrying a torch for your aunt!'

I gaped at her, unable to think of anything to say. Was it possible that after all these years Aunt Thecla might actually find love? Clearly she had before. But that was so long ago and she was so much younger and prettier and so much ... well ... so much *less* like the person she was today.

Tansy just grinned. 'He didn't deny it when I asked him, you know.'

'Why? What did he say?'

'That I'm as bad as Mum for jumping to conclusions! But he didn't say it *wasn't* a date!'

I grinned. Then an idea occurred to me. 'Do you know where they're having lunch?'

'The pub at the far end of the village. Why? Do you think we should go and spy on them?'

'Of course not! There's something I need to do while my aunt's out of the way, that's all.'

'What is it? Maybe I can help!'

I told her I needed to sneak into my aunt's house but I didn't say why.

'I'll come with you,' she offered. 'You'll need someone to keep watch in case she comes back early. She might do if she has a row with my dad!'

That seemed like a reasonable possibility but it wasn't the main reason I agreed to let Tansy come. I'd suddenly remembered the painting in Aunt Thecla's art room that I really wanted to show her.

Chapter Twenty-One

'You can stand here and keep watch at the window,' I told Tansy after I'd let us into Aunt Thecla's house with the spare keys. 'I won't be long.' I left her standing by the net curtains in the front room while I hurried to the kitchen.

Placing the notes in a spot that my aunt might actually *believe* she'd overlooked proved harder than I'd first thought. I knew she'd already searched her kitchen for the missing money. I knew she'd taken everything off the kitchen shelf where the tin was kept and even checked behind the radiator under the shelf in case the money had fallen and got stuck there.

After I'd rejected every possible location, I spotted her wellington boots by the back door. OK, so she might have already looked there too, but I couldn't think of anywhere better and I was running out of time.

I found Tansy in the hall, peering at one of my aunt's paintings. 'Is that depressing or what?' she said.

'I know,' I murmured.

The painting depicted a small figure crouched on the ground outside a church. The lower two-thirds of the canvas were mostly grey and black while the upper third had a rainbow in the sky. Aunt Thecla had told me the painting represented hope.

'Yikes!' Tansy exclaimed as she spotted a larger painting of a scary-looking orange cat on the stairs.

I grinned. 'That's the orange version of the purple one she painted for us. Only ours has more evil eyes. Mum and Dad are pretending it got lost in the move.'

'So where's this painting you think might be my dad?' Tansy asked.

I checked my watch. 'We'll have to be quick.'

I led her up to the attic room, where the door was unlocked. 'This is Aunt Thecla's art studio,' I said. As I took her inside I felt a bit guilty but I didn't let that stop me.

Seconds later Tansy was laughing at the pictures of all the nudes. 'Imagine taking off your clothes and having to sit there with all those people staring at you. Would that be embarrassing or what? And why would anyone *want* to paint a bunch of naked people anyway?'

'It's not that big a deal,' I said. 'Loads of famous artists painted nudes. Rubens did and … and … well, there are loads of others.'

Tansy had just spotted the painting of the young man in the field of bluebells. 'OMG! Is this the one?' She let out a half-embarrassed, half-delighted snigger as she went to look more closely at the painting. 'The hair certainly looks the same – not sure about the rest – but I mean, who else can it be?' She was fishing out her phone to take a photograph.

'Hey, you can't do that!' I protested.

'I won't show it to anyone,' she insisted with a grin. 'Except my mum. I'll see if *she* thinks it's Dad. Did I tell you she's home from Africa now? She's coming for a visit at the weekend.'

'Tansy, you can't show her! If my aunt finds out –'

'She won't find out! Come on, Libby … you want to know for sure if it's my dad, don't you?'

'But, Tansy …' I followed behind her down the stairs, feeling a bit sick and wondering how I could ever have thought showing her that picture was a good idea.

'Hi, Bella,' I said nervously as she walked into the kitchen.

It was early afternoon and for the last hour I'd been alone in our house – something that doesn't happen very often. When Mum and Bella had arrived back from their shopping trip they'd both headed out again almost immediately. Mum had gone to the surgery and Bella had gone to the garage to see Sam. Dad and Grace were still out too.

'How dare you tell Sam about that money!' Bella burst out angrily the second she saw me. 'Now he thinks I'm a thief, thanks to you!'

'Oh, Bella, I didn't mean to –'

'Yes you did! Anyway, thanks to *you* we're finished now!'

'Finished?'

'That's right! It's probably just what you wanted, isn't it? You've always been jealous of me! Just because you're such a geek that no boy would ever look twice at you!' Her voice trembled and she turned and ran up the stairs.

At that point her nasty words didn't sink in because I was so shocked by her news. I'd never dreamed Sam would dump her because of what I'd told him.

'How come you've split up? What happened?' I pursued her upstairs, feeling a bit sick.

'Didn't you *hear* what I just said? Doesn't it even *bother* you that you're so unpopular?' she spat out.

'Bella –'

'Sam calls you a lump! Did you know that? He always asks me, "How's Gracie and how's the *Lump*?"'

I frowned. This is what she always does when she gets mad at me. She yells and I stay calm, which makes her even more furious, so she goads me and goads me until she gets me to totally lose it too.

'You're making that up,' I said warily. 'Sam wouldn't say that.'

'How do *you* know what Sam would say? You don't even *know* him! You don't know *any* boys! The way you act you probably never will!'

I know the best thing is to walk away and let Bella calm down when she gets like this. I don't know why I wasn't doing that today – why I couldn't seem to let it go.

'I know Sam wouldn't say that because he's not mean like you!' I told her, sounding a lot more confident than I actually felt.

She laughed scornfully. 'I know why you're defending him! You fancy him, don't you? You've probably been making up some pathetic fantasy about him inside your head, haven't you?'

'Don't be stupid!'

'Then why is your face so red? I bet that's why you went running to him. You want to cause trouble because you're jealous that he's my boyfriend!'

'That's not true!' I snapped hotly.

'Don't lie,' she said with a sneer, looking triumphant now that she knew she'd got to me. 'It's such a cliché! Little sister fancies her big sister's boyfriend and hopes that one day he'll notice her. Do you really think he'd ever look at a pathetic kid like you? He thinks you're really boring and plain and immature … oh, and *fat*!'

That onslaught was too much. I felt myself struggling not to cry at the thought of the two of them saying those things about me behind my back.

'I HATE YOU, BELLA!' I exploded.

'Well, I wish you weren't my sister!' she shouted back at me.

And I ran downstairs not even thinking about where I was going – all I wanted was to get away from her.

As I walked around aimlessly outside, I tried to remember if Bella had ever said anything that nasty to me before. We'd had plenty of rows over the years and we'd told each other countless times that we hated each other. This time felt like the worst though. This one felt really serious.

After a while I started to calm down. Maybe, just maybe, Bella had made up that part about what Sam thought of me. (Usually when we make friends again after a big argument she'll confess to making up most of the nasty things she's said.)

I started to question my own part in the whole thing. Had I been wrong to go and speak to Sam? No way did I mean to destroy their relationship. But I knew people sometimes acted unconsciously, driven by motives they weren't even aware of. Mum had talked to me about it when I'd fallen out really badly with my best friend, Sarah, just before she left. Mum suggested that perhaps I'd picked the fight in order to take back some control – 'I'll leave you before you can leave me' sort of thing – without even being aware of what I was doing.

Did I fancy Sam? Maybe a bit. I remembered how I'd put on make-up before I went to see him. Why had I done that if I hadn't wanted to impress him? But it didn't mean I thought there was any chance he would actually go out with me. After all, he was seventeen and I wasn't even thirteen for another couple of months. And in any case I'd never do that to my sister.

I found myself walking towards Tansy's house.

I needed to take my mind off my fight with Bella, and Tansy was probably the only person who might be able to do that. I could also find out how her dad had got on with Aunt Thecla at lunchtime.

When I got there, all the windows were shut and their car wasn't in the driveway. I still rang the doorbell but I didn't hang around when there was no response. I didn't want to go back home yet, so I started to walk further up the road to the little park where I'd been meaning to take Grace.

The playground was deserted. I decided to walk across the fields towards the wooded area. I knew St Clara's was on the other side of those woods because Aunt Thecla had told me how she'd walked this way to school every morning when she was my age.

As I approached the fence that separated the woods from the field I saw a stile and a wooden sign saying *Public Footpath*. When I'd suggested to Bella that maybe in the summer we could walk to school this way, she said there was no way she'd be traipsing across the fields and woods, treading in cowpats and getting bitten by insects. Dad laughed when she said that and called her a typical townie.

Suddenly my phone rang and I was surprised to see Aunt Thecla's name on the screen. Why was she phoning me? Unless … I felt my gut churning nastily as I wondered if she'd just found the fifty pounds.

Chapter Twenty-Two

Fifteen minutes later I stood outside my aunt's house and nervously rang the bell. As soon as she came to the door I thought she looked different, and at first I couldn't work out why. Then I realised what it was. She was wearing make-up, something she hardly ever does, and I could see she'd had her hair done.

'Aunt Thecla, you look really ... *nice!*' I gasped, unfortunately managing to sound like that was most unusual. (A crumpliment Dad would call it.)

My aunt flushed. 'Well, I've just been out to lunch.'

'With Tansy's dad. I know. How did it go?'

'Actually, I had a very nice time.' Now she was the one making it sound like the 'nice' part had been unexpected. She looked thoughtful as she continued, 'I'd forgotten how much fun Michael and I used to have together when we were young, before ... well ... anyway, he reminded me of all sorts of things I hadn't thought about in years.'

'The picnics you had in the bluebell woods?' I suggested.

She looked amused rather than surprised by my knowledge. 'I gather Tansy's been telling you quite a lot. That's why I thought I ought to have a little chat with you ... I must say that I haven't thought about Michael very much over the years.'

'But you've still got that painting of him up on your wall!' I blurted out before I could stop myself. When she frowned as if she honestly didn't know what I was talking about, I added, 'We saw it in your art room, remember. The one of him in the field of bluebells.'

'Oh, but that isn't Michael!'

'But ... but ... his hair's just the same and ...' I only just stopped myself from saying that even Tansy thought it looked like her dad.

She was shaking her head emphatically. 'Michael never had hair quite like that, although he did let it grow longer when he was away at university ...' She paused. 'It's his brother, Murray, who's in the painting.'

'Murray who died?' I was a bit taken aback.

'Yes. He christened me Bluebell one spring when I was

185

about your age. I always spent hours in the field and the woods by the school, sketching and painting the bluebells.'

I didn't know what to say. I hadn't thought of my aunt as being close to Murray, but then I guess it made sense that she'd know him fairly well since they'd all grown up together.

'So did you paint him like that because that's how he dressed?' I asked, thinking he must have been rather a weird young man to wander around in the woods wearing nothing but a sarong around his waist.

She smiled. 'I did that picture of him after he died. I used a photo he'd given me from his trip to Malaysia the year before. He was wearing a sarong in that. Then I decided to put the bluebells in the background rather than the beach. I suppose I wanted to remember him on home ground.' While we were chatting she led me into the kitchen. 'Sit down, Elisabeth,' she said. 'I need to talk to you.'

'What about?' I asked curiously, because it didn't sound as if she'd found the money. I noticed that her wellington boots hadn't been moved from their position by the back door.

'I know Tansy's told you why your dad was expelled

from school,' she began. 'I want to tell you something about that.' She paused. 'You see, that day when he was caught inside the Godwins' house –'

'You were there with Michael,' I finished for her. 'He went to the house to warn you. He already told me.'

She shook her head. 'I know that's what your dad thinks … that's what I told him … but I wasn't there that afternoon. I've just explained it to Michael. I was actually at the airport with Murray.'

'*Murray?*' I certainly hadn't seen that one coming. 'But … but *why?*'

'Because I was in love with him. I had been ever since he'd come home from Malaysia a few months earlier. But I was already engaged to Michael so I didn't know what to do. I was so confused. I didn't dare tell him, or anyone else. My mother had died by then and there was nobody else I could confide in. Then on the day Murray left for India I panicked. I desperately wanted to tell him how I felt before he left. So I called a taxi to take me to the airport, and I told Paul I was going to see Michael so that he'd cover for me with our father.'

'Oh …' I murmured as I thought about Dad's version of the story. 'So was that why you couldn't stand up for Dad when he got caught?'

'Yes. I didn't want the truth getting out about where I'd been. I was rather harsh to your dad at the time, but I was feeling so awful myself when I got back from the airport …'

'What happened at the airport?' I asked curiously. 'Did you tell Murray how you felt? What did he say?'

'He told me he was very flattered and that he loved me too, but purely as you would love a younger sister. He was very sweet to me. He said maybe I shouldn't rush into getting married to Michael or anyone else just yet. I waited with him until he had to go through into the departure lounge. He gave me a hug and said, "Don't worry, Bluebell. Everything will be all right. You'll see."' She stared into the distance for several seconds. 'I'm glad I told him how I felt.' Then she turned her back to me as she made herself a cup of tea. She took a little while to do it.

I sat there waiting until she looked at me again. Then I asked gently, 'Is that why you broke off your engagement?'

She nodded. 'Michael was my best friend, but how could I marry him when all I could think of was his brother? Poor Michael took it very badly. I felt terrible, but I couldn't tell him the reason – just that I'd changed my mind.'

There was a bit of a silence while I thought about

everything she'd said. 'Dad never talks about Murray,' I finally murmured. 'But then I guess he wasn't as close to him as you were.'

'Oh, but he was! Murray was like the older brother he'd never had. Michael used to get quite jealous of how close the two of them were. Murray taught your dad how to play cricket, and he let him ride around with him on his beloved motorbike and –'

'Wait – did you just say Dad rode a motorbike?' I said incredulously.

'He rode pillion on Murray's bike all the time, yes.'

'But he's always telling us motorbikes are really dangerous!'

'Yes ... well, you see I don't think he's ever really got over what happened to Murray.'

I frowned. 'What did happen exactly? Tansy said he died in India but she didn't say how.'

'He was killed on the road. He'd bought himself a second-hand motorbike out there and he planned to tour the whole country on it. But his bike was involved in a collision with a truck.'

'That's awful,' I gasped.

She nodded. 'Paul never talks about it. Sometimes I think he should, but ... it's up to him.'

I watched her as she came to sit down with me at the table, bringing a tin of biscuits. I kept quiet as she opened the tin and offered me one. I was going to refuse but then I saw she had KitKats.

'That must be why Dad hates motorbikes,' I said, 'and why he gets so angry if he sees one being driven too fast.'

My aunt nodded. 'I believe Murray used to ride his bike rather fast – egged on by your dad, no doubt. Your dad used to love riding with him. He had no fear at all in those days!'

I stared at her in disbelief, remaining silent as I unwrapped my KitKat and tried to get my head round this new version of Dad.

'So are you and Michael friends again now?' I asked her after the silence had gone on for a while.

She gave me a little smile. 'I hope so. We've agreed to put the past behind us and just enjoy getting to know each other again.' She paused. 'I must say it's nice that you and Tansy have become friends. It feels very … *healing*.'

I nodded, glad that she felt that way. 'But you and Dad need to sort things out as well,' I said. 'You should probably tell him what you just told me.'

'I will – as soon as he starts speaking to me again. But

I don't want *you* to tell him before I do. I think it needs to come from me.'

'Of course, but, Aunt Thecla …' I frowned, not wanting her to take my question the wrong way. 'I don't really understand why you're telling all this to *me*.'

'Oh, well,' she replied crisply. 'I know what you're like for nosing about in the past, Libby. And quite frankly I'd rather you got your facts straight from the horse's mouth, rather than relying on Tansy Godwin for information about our family.'

'Ah …' I smiled – at least that much made sense.

★ Chapter Twenty-Three

Aunt Thecla sounded a lot less friendly when she rang me on my mobile the next morning. Though I suppose I should have been glad she phoned me rather than going straight to Dad, as she probably would if they hadn't fallen out. I'd been in the bathroom so I hadn't picked up, thank goodness, but she'd left me a terse message saying that she'd just found fifty pounds inside her wellington boot. She added that she was coming round to speak with us all tonight, and that she would also leave a message for Mum to inform her of that.

'Bella, what are we going to tell her?' I said as I got dressed in our bedroom while she continued to laze in bed. We'd been ignoring each other until now, and for once I hadn't felt like being the first to break the silence. The only reason I was speaking to her now was because I figured this was an emergency.

After I'd let her hear the message she'd continued to keep her back to me, and now she snapped, 'Don't ask me! You're the one who had to go and put the money back and get yourself caught. You could have left things how they were and everything would have blown over. But oh no ... Libby had a better idea ...' She turned her head then and I saw that her eyes were a bit puffy like she'd been crying. I knew she was worried because she hadn't heard from Sam yet.

'Maybe we should just tell her the truth?' I suggested. 'We don't need to say why you took the money.'

'No way are we telling them the truth!' She glowered at me.

I sighed, sensing that I wasn't going to get anywhere while she was angsting over Sam. 'Bella, you and Sam will be OK ...' I began.

'Oh yeah?' She turned on me angrily. 'How do *you* know?'

'Well, have you tried phoning *him*?' The trouble with Bella is that she never wants to be the one who backs down.

'Of course! It keeps going straight to voicemail. He doesn't want to speak to me.' She sniffed.

'Oh ...' That kind of surprised me, but I had other things to worry about. 'Maybe he just needs a bit more time to come round, but, Bella, listen … Aunt Thecla's going to want an explanation about the money. If I don't tell her the truth, what *am* I going to say?'

She shrugged. 'You're so clever … I'm sure you'll think of something. Now can you please just go away and give me some privacy?'

I left our bedroom wondering why she always seemed to take priority whenever we both wanted a place to retreat to.

Downstairs Dad was cleaning the kitchen floor while Grace sat in the living room with the TV turned up really loud. She'd been allowed to watch loads more TV since we came here. Basically, whereas Mum tries to limit the TV, Dad likes to use it as a sort of babysitter so he can get on with his own stuff.

I knew I needed to plan what I was going to say to Aunt Thecla about her money. I thought about whether I should go to her house and just tell her the truth – or a variation of it. But what could I tell her we'd needed the money for that would sound convincing? It had to be something Mum and Dad wouldn't buy for us or lend us the money for.

Feeling like I needed to escape for a while I decided to go and see Tansy.

*   *   *

I arrived at my new friend's house wondering how much her dad had told her about his lunch with my aunt. I'd already texted her to see if it was OK to come round, and as soon as I rang the bell she came to the door.

'Dad's on the phone with my mum,' she said immediately, looking more tense than I'd ever seen her. 'I told you she's back in the country, didn't I?'

'Yes, Tansy! That's brilliant!'

'Well, I'm really mad at her. She can't have it both ways. First she's desperate to leave me to go and set up a clinic in Africa, and now she's desperate to have me back like nothing ever happened! Well, she can't treat me like that!' She started up the stairs, and when I didn't immediately follow she turned back and snapped, 'Come on, then!'

I hurried after her feeling confused. 'Wait a minute, are you saying your mum wants you to go back and live with her in Southampton?' I asked as I caught up with her in her room.

Her bedroom resembled an old-fashioned guest room rather than the bedroom of an almost-teenage girl. Her stuff seemed to be dumped around the floor in various boxes, as if she wasn't planning on staying long enough to bother unpacking.

195

'Yes, but I already told her I wasn't ever going to move back in with her, and I meant it!' she said as she flopped down heavily on her bed. 'I mean, why should she get away with just walking out on me like that? She has to face the consequences of what she did, right?'

'OK ...' I paused, worried by something I couldn't quite put my finger on. 'But you do actually *want* to stay here with your dad, right?'

'It doesn't matter what I want,' she said dismissively.

'I don't get it. Why wouldn't it matter?'

'Look,' she said impatiently. 'I love Dad, but I've always been a lot closer to Mum. I miss her really badly and I miss our old life in Southampton. So what I *want* is to have that life back, but it's not that simple.'

'Oh ...' I was too surprised to respond for a few moments. Then I said, 'Why isn't it?'

'I just told you! Mum can't leave me behind like I don't matter and then expect me to go running back to her whenever it suits her.'

I must have stayed silent for too long because she suddenly looked at me closely and asked, 'You *do* get that, right?'

I nodded quickly. 'Of course I get it.' I actually tend to get most people's points of view in most situations, which makes it hard to take sides sometimes when there's a disagreement.

'So you'd do the same if you were me?'

'I don't know … maybe … it's just … aren't you sort of cutting off your nose to spite your face?'

She gave a dismissive little huff. 'I don't care.'

There was an awkward silence because I didn't know what else to say. I knew she was lying about not caring. But I wasn't sure if she actually *knew* she was lying. I decided to change the subject.

'Did your dad say anything to you about his lunch with my aunt?' I asked.

I wondered if he'd told her about Aunt Thecla confessing over lunch that she'd been in love with his older brother.

Tansy shook her head. 'He's been acting a bit weird since though, like something's bugging him. I thought maybe their lunch date didn't go so well. Did your aunt say anything about it to you?'

'A bit,' I said, avoiding her gaze.

'You know, he's been talking a lot about that day my grandfather caught your dad with Murray's cricket bat. He says he feels really guilty about it because he knew Murray meant your dad to have it. He was jealous, so that's why he didn't say anything. And guess what? He was clearing out Grandpa's garage the other day and –'

But she didn't have time to finish because from downstairs her dad suddenly yelled, 'TANSY!' at the top of his voice. When we came out on to the landing he was looking up at us from the hall. 'Oh, I didn't realise you were here, Libby. I need to talk to Tansy about something. It might take a while ...'

'Oh, sure.' I know when to take a hint and I instantly headed for the front door.

'I'll text you later!' she called out after me.

As I walked home I tried to imagine myself in Tansy's situation. How would I feel if Mum left *me* for several months to go and set up a clinic in Africa? I would miss her so badly, though I'm sure I'd also be really proud of her and boast to everyone I met about what she was doing. Tansy sounded more outraged than anything else – outraged that her mum hadn't put her first. I suppose it could be because she's an only child and accustomed to being the centre of her mum's world all the time. But then again ... Mum says you have to be careful not to judge other people, or jump to conclusions about them, before you've actually walked in their shoes for a while. And since I'd never been in the situation Tansy was in right now, I guess I didn't really know how I'd react if I ever was.

I was surprised when my phone pinged before I'd even got home. The message from Tansy said: *OMG! Mum visiting tomorrow!*

I wasn't sure how to respond since I didn't know whether the OMG was an excited OMG or a horrified one. That's the trouble with texting. Sometimes you need to see the other person's facial expression and hear their tone of voice as well.

I texted back: *Good luck!* which I hoped sounded both neutral and interested.

The trouble was I was starting to feel a bit worried on my own behalf now I knew Tansy's mum wanted her to go back to Southampton with her. Because I really didn't want to have to start at my new school on my own.

Chapter Twenty-Four

That afternoon I decided to go and meet Mum from work.

I had to wait for her to finish her clinic, and as soon as she saw me standing at reception she asked, 'Libby, darling, is anything wrong?' It made me realise that I'd never surprised her by meeting her from work before. Maybe I should do it more often now that it was within walking distance.

'I just wanted to walk you home,' I said. 'And talk to you on your own.'

'Really? Well, let's go.'

As we set off along the street together she asked, 'So what have you been up to today?'

'I went round to Tansy's. Her mum's just got home – she's a doctor who's been working for a charity in Africa. She went to set up a health clinic and train local nurses in a very poor village.'

'That sounds amazing,' Mum said.

'Yes, but it must be awful not to see your mum for four months. I guess you can understand why Tansy's so angry with her, can't you?' When she didn't answer immediately, I said, 'I mean, *you'd* never go away and leave us for that long, would you?'

I was surprised when she said, 'To be honest, I don't know. If Grace was older ... well ... the chance to make that sort of difference doesn't come around very often.'

'So you think it's OK for Tansy's mum to just go off and leave her?'

'I'm just saying that these decisions aren't always as black and white as they appear. After all, she's being a wonderful role model for Tansy.'

We walked along in silence for a bit as I thought about it. Maybe she had a point. Though I doubted Tansy would ever see it that way.

'So did you want to talk to me about something in particular?' Mum asked.

'Um ...' Now that the time had come I wasn't sure I could actually do it.

'Does this have anything to do with the call I had from Aunt Thecla this morning?' she prompted me. 'She's coming round after dinner tonight to talk to us. She wouldn't tell me much but she says it's about her missing money. I haven't told your dad yet.'

I swallowed, knowing I couldn't put it off any longer. So I took a deep breath and told her the truth. 'I put back Aunt Thecla's fifty pounds and she's just found it.'

Mum stopped walking and stared at me. 'Are you telling me it was *you* who took it?'

'No,' I said quickly.

She gave me a narrow-eyed look. 'Then who did?'

I shook my head. 'I can't tell you …'

Mum sounded annoyed as she said, 'That's not how it works, Libby. If you don't want to be held accountable then you have to tell me what you know. Was it Grace? Because if you think you're doing her a favour by covering up for her –'

'It wasn't Grace!' I protested, and instantly I could see that she'd never really thought it was.

'So it was Bella!' she stated firmly. (After all, it's not rocket science. Not when there are only three of us.)

'Yes,' I said shakily. 'But, Mum, she needed the money really badly.'

'What for?'

I knew that if I told the truth then everything would come crashing down. Sam would be in trouble as well as

Bella, and the two of them might be separated forever and never get a chance to make up. Plus Bella would hate me – and I mean *really* hate me.

'I can't tell you,' I said.

Mum's eyes went cool. 'Then I shall have to ask Bella.'

We walked the rest of the way home in complete silence.

If Mum had been a better investigator (I mean of something other than people's flossing habits) she'd have stopped me from rushing upstairs to talk to Bella the second we got in. After all, you only have to watch any detective show on TV to know that you never let suspects talk to each other before you interrogate them.

So while Mum was in the kitchen recounting everything in a stressed-out voice to Dad, I was in our bedroom warning Bella that Mum knew she'd taken the money. And that she needed to come up with a *really* good reason for needing fifty pounds. And that she needed to come up with it *fast*.

A few minutes later Dad's voice was yelling up the stairs, 'BELLA! GET DOWN HERE! NOW!'

Mum and Dad shut themselves in the living room with Bella while I went into the kitchen to join Grace, who was sitting drawing at the table.

'Mummy says Aunt Thecla is on her way round,' she informed me without looking up.

'Oh *great*,' I said.

At least Dad and our aunt were speaking to each other again, even if it wasn't under the best of circumstances. Prompted by Mum, I'd apologised to Aunt Thecla for not telling her the truth about the money and then been dispatched to help Grace get ready for bed. Bella was interrogated for ages, and by the time they finally released her I was already in bed. She came into our room looking exhausted.

'So …' I murmured nervously. 'Do they know about Sam?'

'Of course not!' She sniffed. 'I told them I wanted the money to get my hair dyed pink before we started school.'

'What?' I started to laugh.

She grinned too. 'I said I wanted to stand out from the other girls.'

'Oh, Bella, that's brilliant!' Not only was it totally believable that my sister would do something like that, but it also made sense that she couldn't have gone to Mum and Dad to borrow the money. 'But wait … didn't they ask why you hadn't used your own money?' I was thinking about her savings, which I knew she'd given to Sam.

She nodded. 'I told them I spent everything on a really expensive goodbye gift for Sam.' Bella has always been able to think on her feet – and lie convincingly if she has to.

'So are they really mad at you?' I asked.

'Aunt Thecla definitely is. Mum and Dad were so relieved I hadn't gone through with the hair-dyeing thing that it sort of took the edge off it! Though they've taken away my phone again and I'm grounded for the rest of the holidays.'

'What about me?' I asked nervously.

'Oh, I told them you didn't know I'd taken the money until afterwards, and that as soon as you found out you insisted we had to put it back.'

'Thanks, Bella.'

She shrugged. 'Well, thanks for not telling them about Sam.'

I paused. 'Have you heard from him yet?'

'No. I was going to go and find him at the garage tomorrow but I can't do that now …'

'I'll go to the garage for you,' I said quickly. 'I can give him a message.'

'Would you?'

'Of course! I'll go first thing tomorrow morning. You could write him a note.'

'Thanks, Libby. Listen … about all that stuff I said to you when we argued … you know I didn't mean any of it, right?'

I sighed. 'I hoped you didn't.'

'I'm sorry. I just get so angry sometimes that it all spills out.'

Chapter Twenty-Five

The following morning the atmosphere felt very tense. I had to be careful not to make Dad suspicious by seeming too desperate to leave the house, but finally I was on my way to the village garage, planning what I was going to say to Sam. I had the letter from Bella in my pocket but I wanted to add my own plea for him to get in touch with her soon.

I reached the garage and saw Bill working on a car out front. As I walked towards him I looked around for Sam but couldn't spot him. 'Hello,' I said shyly. 'Where's Sam?'

Bill looked up, wiping his hands on a rag. 'His last day was yesterday.'

'Oh.' I hadn't expected that.

'Have you tried his phone?'

'My sister has but it's going to voicemail.'

'Ah …' Bill nodded. 'Can't help you then. Sorry.'

As I walked along the road I tried Sam's phone again

and left a message asking him to call me back. Either he'd gone home – which I guess he might have done if he thought he and Bella were finished – or he was still staying at Rat Cottage.

I went back to our house to collect my bicycle and helmet from the shed, and managed to do it without alerting Dad.

Soon I was cycling along the country road that led to the cottage. Thankfully it wasn't busy, except for a motorbike whizzing past me. I thought about how Dad always grunts his disapproval whenever a motorbike passes him at high speed. 'He's going to get himself killed,' he always says angrily. One time he really embarrassed Bella and me by winding down his window at the traffic lights to speak to a handsome young biker who'd just overtaken us. 'Hey, you! Watch your speed! You're not invincible, you know!'

Dad's dislike of motorbikes made total sense now that I knew about Murray. I wanted to ask him more about it but I knew I'd have to wait for the right time. I could still hardly imagine him, even as a teenager, riding on the back of Murray's bike, urging him to go faster.

I eventually came to the road the cottage was on. Halfway along it was the track we'd followed before – the one that led to the abandoned den. I decided to go and see if Sam's bike was there. If it wasn't, it meant that he was out for the day or gone for good, and either way there was no point in me going to look for him at the cottage.

It felt a bit spooky walking into the woods on my own. I left my bike leaning against a tree and soon found the den, feeling relieved when I saw Sam's motorbike there.

Five minutes later I arrived at Rat Cottage, glad to see no cars parked there, no dogs and no sign of anyone about. Since I didn't want to attract the attention of any passers-by I rested my bike against the wall and hurried round the back.

The back room had old sash windows that were easily opened from the outside if the frames were jiggled a bit. Mum had demonstrated it to Dad when she'd been fretting about how easily a burglar could get in – if Dad happened to be wrong about the non-existence of crime in the countryside. But today I couldn't seem to get the frames to budge. Maybe the wood had swollen in the rain, or the frames had been nailed shut after we'd left.

I rapped on the glass as loudly as I dared, then went to knock on the back door. 'SAM? ARE YOU IN THERE? IT'S LIBBY!'

When that didn't meet with any response I stepped back and looked at the upstairs windows for any sign of him. All the curtains were closed. I took out my phone to call him and saw that, as usual, I had no signal. I hadn't forgotten how intermittent the phone reception was here, and I knew it might be the reason Sam wasn't answering Bella's calls, though it didn't explain why he wasn't picking up her messages whenever he left the cottage.

I decided to try the front of the house instead. I was approaching the front door when I heard a sound I'd become a lot more familiar with since we'd moved to the country. First I heard the clip-clop of hooves on the road, and then I turned to see three horses walking around the bend. And even in their riding hats I recognised Katie and the two girls I'd met at the park.

I instantly had butterflies in my tummy. What were they doing here?

'Look who's here!' the one called Fran exclaimed.

Katie dismounted, handing the reins to Fran, who thankfully seemed to be staying on her horse. Katie was looking at me curiously. She sounded quite friendly as she asked in a teasing voice, 'You're not *still* looking for your Frisbee, are you?'

I shrugged. 'Nothing else to do here.' Goodness knows why I said that!

Katie's horse suddenly did a massive poo on the road.

I'm sure I didn't react with anything except slight surprise but Fran instantly decided that I was disgusted by it.

'There's no need to turn your nose up,' she mocked. 'It's only digested grass. It's not nearly as gross as *your* poo.'

The other girl – Lara – giggled. Since I didn't quite know how to respond I decided to ignore them.

'When are your aunt and uncle back?' I asked Katie in as casual a voice as I could manage.

'Next week.' She was unlocking her aunt's front door by this time. 'I've got to water the plants. I'll be out in a minute.'

I was going to leave, but I couldn't help giving her horse a quick pat. I love horses. I'd asked Mum if I could have riding lessons now that there were stables just along the road, but she'd said we didn't have the budget for them at the moment. 'Wait until your birthday,' she said. 'Then we'll see.'

I forgot about everything for a moment as I reached up and stroked the neck of Katie's horse, rubbing the rough but glossy coat and breathing in the distinctive horsey smell. 'She's really beautiful,' I said admiringly as I stroked the animal's long black nose.

'*He*,' Fran corrected me with a bit of a sneer. She pointed at the horse's undercarriage and added, 'Or don't they teach you about the difference between girls and boys at those posh schools?'

The two of them burst out laughing and I blushed bright red, which made me feel even more stupid. Of course my old school (which wasn't posh in any case) had done the whole sex education syllabus. I just wasn't in the habit of bothering to correctly identify the gender of horses before I patted them, that's all.

'They don't *have* any boys at St Clara's, remember,' Lara pointed out. 'Maybe she really doesn't know the difference!'

As Fran sniggered all I could think about was getting away from them as fast as I could. I rushed to get on my bike, hoping that Sam would keep quiet and stay inside until they left – presuming he actually *was* inside. If he'd gone out for a walk I just hoped he stayed away until the coast was clear.

As I cycled back down the lane I knew Bella would be waiting anxiously at home for news, and I wished I had something more to tell her. I suddenly remembered that I still had her letter for Sam. I should have put it through the letterbox at the cottage, but I couldn't go back and do it while Katie and her pals were there.

I decided I'd just have to return to the cottage later. Hopefully by then Sam would be back. After all, he couldn't be far away – not while his bike was still here.

Chapter Twenty-Six

Lunch at home was pretty tense. Mum was at work as usual, so Dad was in charge. Bella was barely speaking to anyone, and although she didn't get cross with me when I explained about Katie and her friends, she was upset to hear that I hadn't managed to see Sam.

We finished eating the fish-finger sandwiches Dad had made and I was helping clear the table when I got a text from Tansy. 'She wants to know if I can go round to hers this afternoon,' I told Dad. 'That's OK, isn't it?'

'I should think so. But if you want to go anywhere else from there you need to let me know.'

'*Why?*' Bella protested in a pained sort of voice. 'I thought you said the country was safer than the town!'

'Don't you start with that tone of voice, young lady,'

213

Dad snapped at her, far more forcefully than he usually does.

'OK, Dad,' I said quickly, realising that with the mood he was in I'd have to be careful how I handled him.

Tansy must have been waiting for me because the second I set foot on her front porch she flung open the door and pulled me inside. 'Guess who's here?' she said excitedly.

'Your mum?'

'No! Well, yes, she's here too … but I meant your aunt!'

'OK …' I wasn't sure where this was going so I waited to hear more.

'Dad invited her round to look at some stuff he found when he went through the garage – stuff that belonged to Murray.'

'Tansy!' called out an unfamiliar female voice. An attractive woman of about Mum's age walked into the hall. She was slim with dark hair and she wore a white blouse tucked into blue trousers.

'Mum, this is Libby,' Tansy introduced me at once.

'Hello, Libby,' the woman said with a friendly smile. 'I've heard a lot about you.' She turned to Tansy. 'Darling, I must go and check in to my hotel but we can talk more this evening.' She leaned forward and kissed Tansy on her forehead, then pulled her close and hugged her tightly. 'I don't want you to worry. Everything will be fine, whatever you decide. You know Daddy and I both just want you to be happy.'

I half expected Tansy to say that if that were true then she shouldn't have disappeared off to Africa for four months, but instead Tansy murmured, 'OK, Mum,' seeming only too pleased to have such a big fuss made of her.

As we watched her mum walk down the drive and on to the street where she'd left her car I asked, 'Did you tell her how bad you felt about her going away?'

Tansy nodded. 'It's sort of difficult *not* to tell her how I feel about stuff. If I'm ever worried or in a bad mood about anything, she always picks up on it and asks me about it.' Her eyes suddenly went a bit shiny with tears, as if she was finally letting herself feel how much she'd been missing her mum.

'So what are you going to do now?' I asked.

'I don't know. She really wants me to go back to Southampton with her.'

'Can't *she* move *here* instead?' I suggested hopefully.

Tansy shook her head. 'Her job is there.'

'What does your dad say about it?'

'That it's up to me.'

Before I could say anything else she swiftly changed the subject. 'Come on. Dad's got something to show you. We need to tell him you're here.'

Five minutes later I was walking to the garage at the side of the house with Tansy, her dad and Aunt Thecla. I tried to sneak a look at my aunt to see how much she knew, but her face was giving away nothing.

'I found some of my brother's old things in here, Libby, and there's something I'd like you to look at,' Tansy's dad said as he unlocked the garage door.

Aunt Thecla suddenly placed her hand on my shoulder and said, 'Michael wants to give this to your father because he thinks that's what Murray would have wanted. I'm not so sure though. I wanted to see what you thought about it first.'

I was certain then that I knew what it was they had found.

'I'm sure Dad would love to have Murray's cricket bat,' I said without hesitation. 'I think it would mean a lot to him.'

'Oh, but we're not talking about the cricket bat,' my aunt said as Tansy's dad opened the garage door and stepped aside.

I just stared. Because there, standing among a whole lot of other junk, was a very old-fashioned and very rusty-looking motorbike.

Chapter Twenty-Seven

'It belonged to my uncle Murray,' Tansy said, though of course I'd already guessed that much.

'What do you think, Libby?' Mr Godwin asked. 'Will your father want it?'

'Um ...' I couldn't stop staring at the dirty black pillion seat, which was now cracked on the surface with the foam showing in places. I just couldn't imagine Dad as a sixteen-year-old actually riding on it.

'I told Michael this afternoon that I trust your opinion on this as much as anybody's, Libby,' Aunt Thecla added.

'You do?' To be honest it was a bit of a shock to be selected by my aunt for my opinion on something so important.

'I wouldn't say it if I didn't mean it, Libby,' she said impatiently. 'So what do you think?'

'Well, it's a nice idea,' I began slowly, 'but Dad usually

gets pretty freaked out about motorbikes. I'm not sure he'd actually want to *own* one.'

'But this is a bit different, don't you think?' Mr Godwin said. 'This has sentimental value. Besides, I'm sure it could be restored and sold for quite a bit of money if he didn't want to keep it himself at the end of the day.'

I looked at the bike again, wondering if Dad would see it as an old friend rather than just another dangerous motorbike that he didn't want to let us anywhere near. I thought about how he never talks about his friendship with Murray, almost as if he doesn't want to think about it because of all the painful memories. Maybe seeing Murray's old bike would make him feel really sad. On the other hand, maybe seeing it would trigger some good memories from before Murray died. Maybe it would remind him of all the good times they'd had together.

'I think we should probably tell him about the bike and let him decide if he wants it or not,' I said.

'You don't think he'll be upset?' Aunt Thecla asked.

'I *do* think he'll be upset,' I said carefully. 'But maybe not *just* upset.'

There was a bit of a pause. Then Mr Godwin said, 'OK, Libby. We'll tell your dad the bike's here and that he can have it if he wants it. I just need to know one way or the other before I sell this house.' As he spoke we saw a van pulling up outside.

'Expecting someone?' Aunt Thecla said.

'Oh, that'll be Bill from the garage. I phoned him about the bike this morning. I want to get his opinion on what state it's in and he said he'd come by and take a look.'

'Bill from the garage in the village?' I asked in alarm.

'Yes. He's an excellent mechanic. My father swore by him.'

'Do you know him, Libby?' my aunt asked.

But Bill was already walking up the drive towards us. I was panicking inside, hoping he wouldn't recognise me or say anything about Sam. Thankfully he didn't speak to any of us as his attention was grabbed by the bike.

'It's an old Bantam,' he said as he started to look it over. When he tried the kick-starter lever we were all astonished when the engine actually worked. But as soon as he turned the handlebar on one side to rev it up it cut out.

'I'm surprised it started at all,' Tansy's dad said. 'It must have been sitting there for thirty years or more.'

'I can take it to the garage if you like,' Bill said. 'I can do a bit of work on it, see if I can get it running.' He glanced at me then. 'It's a job young Sam would've been interested in, I reckon. It's a pity I didn't have enough work to keep him on. A good lad, that one.'

I gulped.

'Wait … did you say *Sam*?' Aunt Thecla asked sharply.

Bill nodded. 'That's right – the young lad who's been helping me out for the last couple of weeks. Pity he's no family about here to look out for him. The lass here knows him.' He looked at me with a twinkle in his eye. 'But I'm guessing not as well as that older lass, eh?'

'Umm …' I felt myself blushing furiously. What on earth could I say now?

'Elisabeth?' Aunt Thecla's voice demanded an answer. 'This isn't the Sam I'm thinking of, is it?'

It did cross my mind that I could always ask which Sam she *was* thinking of. But in the end I decided there wasn't much point.

'He came here to be with Bella,' I mumbled.

Aunt Thecla was glaring at me. 'Do your parents know?' She narrowed her eyes even more. 'Don't bother to answer that. Of course they don't.'

Neither of us spoke as we walked back together – not after I made it clear that I wasn't going to tell her anything else.

'Where do you think you're going?' she demanded as I went to fetch my bicycle from out the back the second we got home.

'To get some fresh air,' I told her as I grabbed my helmet.

'Not right now you're not!'

But I ignored her. I knew it was only a matter of time before the whole story about Sam came out, including where he was staying. The best thing I could do now was to go and warn him.

I just hoped he'd be there this time.

Nothing about the cottage had changed since this morning. The curtains were still closed and there was no sign of anyone there.

This time I walked right up to the front door and banged on it as loudly as I could. 'SAM! IT'S LIBBY! IF YOU'RE THERE, OPEN THE DOOR!'

Straight away I heard a noise inside.

'SAM! LET ME IN!' I yelled impatiently.

A muffled voice sounded from the other side of the door. 'It's not locked!'

So I turned the handle and pushed hard and to my great surprise the door opened.

'Sam!' I called out crossly, but then I gasped.

He was lying by the side of the staircase, bits of wood from the broken banister scattered all around him. His right leg was bent at a strange angle underneath him and I could smell stale vomit where he must have thrown up. His face was white and his hair was stuck to his forehead with sweat. I realised with horror that he'd probably been lying there for a long time. In fact, he might have already been there when I was at the cottage that morning.

'SAM!' I could feel my heart pounding as I rushed over to him. Bella and I had forgotten to warn him about the dodgy railing. I felt terrible as I swiftly took out my phone.

'Hey …' He reached out and grabbed my wrist. 'What are you doing?'

'Calling my dad.'

'No.' He started to cough.

'Sam, I *have* to call him.'

'No!'

'Dad will help you –'

'Kill me … more like … Libby …' He let his head fall back on to the floor again and started to moan. 'I think my leg's broken …'

I glanced down at his leg again and thought that was highly likely. Then I checked my phone – and of course there was no signal! Plus there was no landline in the cottage and the couple next door was still away. That only left the end cottage with the very deaf old lady who never answered her door.

'Listen, I'm going to walk along the road to try and get a signal,' I told him. 'I'll be as quick as I can.'

I was standing on the road trying to remember which direction I needed to head in to get a signal when I heard a car approaching. When I saw who it was I could have cried with relief.

'Dad!' I called out.

As he was parking on the grass verge I rushed back inside to tell Sam. But instead of being relieved that he was about to be rescued he just looked scared. 'Libby ... seriously ... don't leave me alone with him. Promise.'

'Sam, it's OK,' I said. 'Dad gets mad sometimes but his bark's worse than his bite.'

'With *you* maybe,' he mumbled.

I quickly rushed back outside to find Dad stomping towards the front door. 'Bella just told me everything,' he said angrily. And he started ranting on about how he was going to kill Sam when he got his hands on him!

'Dad, calm down ...' I began. 'He'll hear you!'

'GOOD!' he yelled. 'SO WHERE IS HE?'

Chapter Twenty-Eight

We went inside to find Sam slumped flat on the floor, white as a sheet, looking like he might throw up again any second.

'What the –' Dad gulped as he took in the sight, his rage gone in an instant.

'I just found him,' I said, fighting back tears. 'Dad, I think he might have been like this all day. You have to help him.'

Dad carefully stepped over the bits of broken wood. 'OK, Sam ... stay absolutely still ... don't try to move ...'

I sighed with relief, even though I hadn't really doubted Dad would change his tune when he saw Sam like this.

I stood back and watched while Dad crouched down, talking to Sam calmly the whole time, using the same voice he uses when he's giving Grace instructions whenever she's hurt or really scared. 'Come on, son ...

deep breaths … I know it must hurt like hell but I'm going to call an ambulance and you'll soon get something for the pain. Everything will be fine.'

He laid a hand on Sam's forehead as if he was checking his temperature, then he asked him if he'd bumped his head and had a quick check for any injury there. He looked at Sam's leg but he didn't touch it.

Tears were running down Sam's face but he wasn't making a sound as he lay there as tensed up and scared as I'd ever seen him.

'It's a good job we found you,' Dad grunted.

'Before the rats did!' I quipped, trying to get Sam to relax as Dad continued to check him over. 'Don't worry, Sam, you're not hallucinating. Dad really *is* being nice to you.'

Dad swore, and for a moment I thought he was reacting to my bad joke. Then I saw that he was swearing at his phone. 'No reception,' he muttered crossly. 'I can't risk moving him into the car with that leg. He needs an ambulance. Stay here with him, Libby, while I go outside and try to get a signal. I might have to drive down the road.'

I nodded and Sam and I silently watched him go. I briefly wondered if I should hold his hand or offer to mop his brow but decided against it. After all, I wasn't Bella.

As if he could mind-read Sam asked hoarsely, 'Where's Bella?'

'She wanted to come and find you but she's grounded. She's been trying to phone you. She thought you were ignoring her calls.'

'I was … yesterday … wanted her to worry … but today …' He started to cough.'

'It's OK, Sam. I get it. She'll understand.'

I went to stand at the front door where I could watch for Dad. I also badly needed some fresh air. The smell of stale vomit was getting to me a bit. Sam had his eyes closed. He looked exhausted.

'I can't believe you ran away from home to be with Bella,' I said, thinking I should probably keep him talking rather than let him go to sleep. 'It's pretty romantic actually.'

He opened his eyes slightly. 'She offered to come away with me instead,' he muttered.

'She did?' I was astonished.

'Yeah … can't say my Bella doesn't have guts …'

'She's not just *your* Bella,' I grunted. 'And Mum and Dad would never have stopped looking for her if she'd run away.'

He nodded. 'I know. That's why I thought it was

better if we did it this way round. Cos I don't have that problem.'

An hour later Dad and I were following the ambulance to the hospital in Castle Westbury. The paramedics had given Sam an injection to ease the pain but it had clearly hurt a lot when they'd splinted his leg to move him. It was only as he was being lifted into the back of the ambulance that he said drowsily, 'What about my bike?'

'What bike?' Dad asked.

'His motorbike. It's hidden in the woods,' I said quickly.

Dad's eyes narrowed but he kept his voice calm as he said, 'Well, it can stay where it is for now. We'll meet you at the hospital, Sam.'

In the car Dad asked, 'Has Bella been riding that bike?'

I didn't reply, which pretty much told him the answer. He shot me a glare, then set about extracting every shred of information from me that he could, including the length of time Sam had been in the cottage and whose idea that had been. When I asked if Sam would get in trouble for squatting, he said that if Mrs Fuller tried to kick up too much of a fuss then *he* would threaten to kick up a fuss about how she'd rented it to us in such a dangerous state in the first place.

At the hospital we waited while a still drowsy Sam was seen by the triage nurse and then a doctor, who sent him for an X-ray and said that his leg was broken and that they would be putting it in plaster and admitting him for the night. Everyone kept assuming Sam was Dad's son, and after a while Dad stopped bothering to correct them.

'I'm going outside to phone your mum and Sam's mother to let them know what's happened,' Dad told me as we waited for Sam to be brought back.

While he was gone I really wished I could phone Bella myself. But of course Bella didn't have her phone and Mum would be on the landline with Dad.

'So did you speak to Sam's mum?' I asked Dad when he reappeared ten minutes later.

'Yes.' He sounded exasperated. 'She says being in hospital is the perfect chance for Sam to apply to social services for emergency housing. Apparently that's what she did herself when she was his age.'

'So she's not coming to see him?'

'Doesn't sound like it.'

'You could try his uncle.'

'I just did. He seemed more interested in the motorbike. Apparently Sam hadn't finished paying him for it when he ran off and he wants it back.'

Just then a nurse came to let us know that Sam was ready to go up to the ward. 'But I still need an address for the admission form,' she said.

I looked at Dad as he jotted down our address in the space Sam had left blank. 'Shouldn't you put "no fixed abode" or something if he wants to apply for emergency housing?' I whispered.

'He isn't fit to be on his own with that leg. He can sleep on the sofa bed in the living room until he's better.'

I was pretty amazed at his change of heart. I mean, I know Dad's a good guy underneath all his huffing and puffing but still ...

Then he added, 'And this way I can keep an eye on him – *and* Bella.' He sighed. 'You know ... Thecla warned me a while back that I was underestimating how strongly they felt about each other ... clearly I should have listened.'

I felt like saying that *of course* he should have listened. Because weirdly enough Aunt Thecla has more experience than any of us when it comes to teenage romance.

Chapter Twenty-Nine

'So, Dad, does this mean you're not too angry with Bella?' I asked tentatively as we drove home.

We'd spent an hour on the ward with Sam, helping him to settle in and making sure he had the stuff he needed. Dad went to the shop to buy him water and chocolate and some toothpaste because he'd run out while he was at the cottage. Sam looked like he was struggling not to cry at one point and Dad had patted him on the shoulder and told him to get some sleep.

'Why would you think that?' Dad grunted.

'Well, you seemed OK with Sam … not angry with him any more, I mean.'

'Sam's in far too fragile a state to cope with my anger on top of everything else. Besides he's been punished enough. Bella is a whole different story. She's got all the family support she could possibly need and yet she's done nothing but go behind our backs, causing trouble ever since we got here.'

'She's been really unhappy, Dad.'

'Not as unhappy as she's going to be. It's time she learnt that it's not just *her* feelings that matter in this family, Libby. When I think how we moved here so she could sit her exams next year at St Clara's, and how she promised never to keep secrets like the bullying from us ever again … and how we trusted her …'

'She didn't *want* to keep Sam a secret, Dad. She felt like she didn't have a choice, because you wanted to split them up. And it's not like *she* wanted to move here or go to St Clara's. She's really nervous about it. She thinks she'll never catch up with the work and that everyone will think she's thick. And she must be really worried about what you're going to do now. She won't guess that you're going to let Sam stay with us. I bet she thinks he's going to get sent back to his mum's.'

'I probably would send him back if she'd have him,' Dad grunted.

I paused, sensing a shred of common ground now.

'His mum doesn't sound very nice,' I said slowly.

'Not a maternal bone in her body, I'd say,' he muttered, shaking his head as if he found her lack of parental concern totally bewildering. 'OK, so she was a kid herself when she had him but she's not a kid any longer. And there are plenty of young mums out there who care a hell of a lot more than that!'

I didn't say anything else. Dad was on Sam's side now, which was all that mattered.

We got home to find Mum in the kitchen making dinner and Grace in the living room doing a jigsaw. I presumed Bella was up in our room, sulking.

'Libby, why don't you help Grace do her jigsaw?' Dad said. 'I need to speak to Mum.'

'Can I go and see Bella first?'

'No. Stay with Grace. I'll talk to Bella after I've spoken to your mother.'

'Libby!' My little sister immediately pulled me over to the table where she'd started to set out a jigsaw that Aunt Thecla had bought for her. It had way too many pieces because our aunt thought she needed 'a bit of a challenge'.

I half expected Bella to come downstairs now we were back. Unless she was lying on her bed with her earphones in and hadn't heard us come in.

After a while Dad went up to speak to her and Mum came through to the living room to tell us dinner was almost ready. We heard Dad calling out Bella's name. Then he shouted down from the landing, 'She's not up here.'

'Well, she's not down here,' Mum said, heading up the stairs to join him.

I started to feel my heart thumping in my chest even before I heard Dad exclaim, 'Wait! There's a note!'

I raced upstairs with Grace close behind wanting to know what was wrong.

I glanced around our bedroom, trying to spot if anything was missing. Bella's rucksack usually hung on a peg on the back of the door along with her summer jacket. Both were gone. And I knew what had happened even before Dad started to read out her note …

Two hours later, Grace had gone to bed and my parents were sitting at the kitchen table looking shattered. Since we'd found out Bella had run away we'd tried everything we could think of to locate her.

Aunt Thecla hadn't seen her or heard from her. I'd phoned Sam at the hospital to see if she'd contacted him, but she hadn't. Dad had even phoned the ward and spoken to a nurse, who confirmed Sam hadn't had any visitors since we'd left. Her bike was still in the shed, so she hadn't cycled anywhere. I just couldn't understand where she'd gone when she was totally without money. That's when I remembered the brooch.

I rushed to check her jewellery box, where I knew she kept it.

'It's not here,' I said.

We started trying to work out how long Bella had been gone. Apparently when Dad had phoned Mum to let her know we were at the hospital with Sam, Bella had begged to be allowed to catch the next bus to Castle Westbury to go and see him. But Mum said no and that she should wait for Dad and me to get back. After that Bella had stayed in her room – or so Mum thought.

'Do you think she's going to try and sell the brooch?' Mum asked me.

'No way!' I said at once. 'She loves that brooch!'

'But she doesn't have any money. Where will she sleep tonight? If only we hadn't confiscated her phone …'

'She wouldn't have answered it, Nina,' Dad said sombrely. 'She's not daft. She must have a plan. And I bet it involves Sam – even if he doesn't know it yet.'

'She might have called him at the hospital already and he's just not telling us,' Mum said.

'How can she call him when she hasn't got her phone?' I pointed out.

'There's such a thing as an old-fashioned telephone box, Libby,' Dad said drily. 'Though come to think of it, would she even know how to use one?'

Mum rubbed her eyes. 'Libby, are you sure you can't think of anywhere else she might have gone? What about that girl you've been hanging out with recently?'

'Tansy? Bella hardly knows her.'

'Phone her anyway, just to check.'

I did, and Mum spoke to Tansy's dad, but they hadn't seen Bella either. Aunt Thecla phoned some of her friends to ask if anyone had seen her in the village that evening, but none of them had. Mum started phoning B & Bs and guest houses in Castle Westbury to see if any girl who sounded like Bella had checked in.

Finally she told me to go to bed. As I lay there I tried to think what I would do if I was Bella. Where would I go? I tried to imagine how she must be feeling and why she'd decided to run away.

I slept fitfully that night, worrying about Bella every time I woke up.

In the morning the first thing I did was run downstairs to see if there was any news. Aunt Thecla was in the kitchen. Mum and Dad had already left the house to look for Bella in Castle Westbury.

'I told them she'll probably come back under her own steam,' Aunt Thecla said. 'After all, she can't very well run off with that boy now he's got a broken leg. It's not like he can whisk her away on the back of his motorbike, is it?'

'Do they think Sam knows where she is?' I asked.

'The boy's not answering his phone apparently. But for sure she'll be at that hospital to see him at some point today. I told them they should just go there and wait.'

I went upstairs and tried Sam's phone myself, but it went straight to voicemail. I started to worry that Bella had already contacted him and that they were planning to run away together. After all, neither of them knew that Dad was willing to let Sam stay at our place. She probably thought she would have to take matters into her own hands if she didn't want to be separated from him.

I tried to think what Bella and Sam might do next. They couldn't ride off into the sunset together on his motorbike, that was for sure. But if Sam was planning to run away with her he would first need to make some sort of arrangement for his bike. I knew he wouldn't just abandon it. In fact, if he couldn't use it himself any more maybe he would even try and sell it.

I threw on some clothes and raced out of the house before Aunt Thecla could ask any questions. I arrived at the garage just as Bill was opening up.

'Bill, have you heard from Sam?' I asked him breathlessly. 'He's broken his leg. I think he'll need some help with his motorbike. Maybe he'll even need to sell it. I thought he might have contacted you about it?'

'No.' He looked puzzled and I immediately felt deflated until he added, 'It would make more sense if he *was* phoning me about that, right enough.'

'What? Wait – so he *has* phoned you?'

'He called last night. One of my customers owns a jewellery shop in Castle Westbury. Sam did a bit of work on her car while he was here. He wanted to know the name of her shop.'

I instantly felt excited. 'Did he say if he wanted to sell some jewellery?'

'Sell? Oh wait …' He was looking worried now. 'She buys antique jewellery, but she won't touch anything dodgy. He's not fencing stuff, is he?'

'Oh no, it's nothing like that!' I said at once. 'It's just

238

my sister's got something she might be trying to sell and she might have asked him to help.'

He told me the name and address of the shop and I rushed back home, knowing I couldn't do the next part on my own. I was going to have to ask Aunt Thecla for help.

Chapter Thirty

Aunt Thecla gave me a lift to the jewellery shop Bill had told me about. First she went inside herself while I waited in the car with Grace. I just hoped we weren't too late. We'd managed to get here half an hour after the shop had opened, but it was still possible Bella had already been and gone.

My aunt came back to the car five minutes later. 'They do buy and sell antique jewellery but nobody has been in there yet this morning. I think I should move the car in case Bella recognises it. I'll leave you here, Libby. She's more likely to listen to you. Grace and I can go to the park.'

'What about Mum and Dad?' I asked, knowing they wouldn't like the fact that we hadn't filled them in on our plan.

'We don't want them interfering and scaring her off,' Aunt Thecla said firmly. 'We'll tell them later.'

'She might not even come,' I said. 'Maybe she's gone to see Sam first.'

'Then your parents will be there waiting for her.' Mum had already phoned to say they were heading for the hospital after failing to find any sign of Bella in town.

'But what if –'

'Do stop procrastinating, Elisabeth! It's a perfectly good plan, so let's get on with it!'

I watched Aunt Thecla drive away with Grace, then I picked a spot to wait for Bella. I wondered which direction she would come from – if she came at all. I was certain she'd have to be feeling really desperate to sell her brooch. It was quite possible she'd already changed her mind.

I found a place behind a parked van a short distance along the road from the shop. Ten minutes later I saw her. I almost shouted out to her in my excitement but I stopped myself. I wanted to get close enough to talk to her without scaring her off, so I waited until she was inside the shop before I followed her.

'Bella!' I called out from the doorway. As she whirled round I said, 'Don't worry. It's just me. I need to talk to you.'

She looked a bit shaken. 'I'll just be a minute,' she told the lady behind the counter. Then she stalked over to grab my arm and march me outside. 'How did you know I was here? Did Sam tell you?'

'No,' I reassured her at once. 'I spoke to Bill at the garage. He said Sam asked him about this place. Mum and Dad don't know. But, Bella, you can't sell your brooch. You love it!'

'Not as much as I love Sam! I have to sell it to pay for a place for us to stay until his leg heals.'

'Bella, listen … Dad's changed his mind about Sam. He says he can come and stay with *us* when he gets out of hospital. He says he underestimated how much you two love each other.'

Bella was scowling suspiciously. 'That doesn't sound like Dad. Anyway, Sam never mentioned it when I spoke to him. Are you sure Mum and Dad haven't put you up to this?'

For some reason her distrust really got to me. I felt anger rise up in my chest, and instead of being my usual submissive self I snapped, 'So what are you saying? That you think I'm *lying*? Because … NEWSFLASH! … I'm actually not that *mean*!'

'I never said you were mean!' she snapped back.

'Good, because *you're* the one who's mean – especially to *me*!'

'It's not my fault if you're way too sensitive!' she said dismissively.

'*Sensitive?* Bella, you told me everyone thinks I'm a dork, and that Sam thinks I'm a *fat lump*!'

'Yeah, well … I already told you I was sorry about that. It's just … sometimes you just need putting down a bit!'

'*WHAT?*'

'You can be such a goody-goody sometimes, Libby! You never get into trouble! Everyone thinks you're so smart! Mum and Dad are so proud of you because you're so clever! At school all the teachers love you! Even Sam says you're really wise for a twelve-year-old! Sometimes it just makes me want to hit you!'

I was totally astounded. Where had all this come from?

'Remember when I told you I felt sorry for you being a middle child?' she continued. 'Well, honestly, Libby, you make being a middle child look like *the* place to be! You're in the middle of everything all the time and everyone in the family tells you stuff – even Aunt Thecla! I bet you *never* feel like an outsider!'

I stared at her. I had no idea she felt this way. It was true that recently I'd come to see that my family *did* value my opinions and seemed to find me easy to talk to. But I'd never realised Bella felt left out. 'But you've always been so cool and confident compared to me!' I grasped at the one fact I knew she couldn't deny. 'And you're so slim and *pretty*! I've always longed to be more like you!'

She scowled. 'Maybe I *am* prettier than you,' she said matter-of-factly, 'but you even managed to trump *that* by looking exactly like Dad and Aunt Thecla's ugly-but-saintly dead mother!'

At that I snorted. I didn't mean to, but it seemed to make Bella see the funny side too. Just as we were both struggling to keep our faces straight my phone started ringing.

When I saw who it was I handed it to Bella. 'It's Dad.'

'I don't want to speak to him,' she grunted.

'Go on, Bella. He'll tell you himself that Sam can stay with us. Besides, they're really worried about you.'

Reluctantly she took the call. I tried not to deliberately listen in but it was pretty obvious that Mum and Dad were both very emotional at the other end, which made Bella get all emotional too. In the end, she put me on the phone to speak to them. I told them that Aunt Thecla was with Grace down the road at the park and that I'd ask her to drive us all to the hospital to meet them.

After I'd phoned our aunt to fill her in I went over to join Bella, who was sitting on a nearby wall. To my horror she was crying.

'Oh, Bella,' I exclaimed as I sat down beside her. I flung my arms around her fiercely, because at the end of the day she was still my sister and I would always love her. I briefly wondered if I needed to remind her of that fact, but then she returned my hug just as fiercely and I knew we were OK.

Sam was discharged from hospital the following day. Dad drove back alone to fetch him. He said he wanted to have a serious man-to-man talk with him on the way home, and that he didn't need any girls interrupting them.

When they finally arrived, Bella held back from flinging herself at Sam while Dad helped him inside the house on his crutches. Sam's leg was encased in thick white plaster up to his thigh.

Dad helped him into the living room, where Bella had made up the sofa bed with loads of extra pillows. In fact, judging by how many she'd used, I doubted the rest of us would have anything to rest our heads on when we went to bed that night.

'Where's Grace?' Dad asked.

'Gone to look at puppies with Aunt Thecla,' I told him. Grace had been trying to persuade her to get another dog ever since we'd got here.

Dad rolled his eyes as he said, 'So what do you think the chances are of her coming back without one?'

As soon as Sam was settled on the sofa with his leg up, Bella flopped down beside him and reached out to tap his plaster cast. 'Does it hurt?'

'Only when you do that,' he said with a grin.

'You need to take your next dose of painkillers,' Dad suddenly remembered. 'I'll get them for you.'

As soon as he'd gone Sam said quietly, 'I've missed you, Bella.'

'I've missed you too. I've been so worried!' She leant over so her face was level with his and for an awful moment I thought they were going to start kissing right there in front of me. But then Bella whispered, 'Where's your bike?'

'I'm going to get Bill to collect it.'

Aha – just as I thought.

'I can't ride with you any more,' Bella told him. 'I promised Dad.'

'I know. He told me.'

Dad came back into the room with a glass of water

246

and a couple of tablets, which he handed to Sam. 'We'll have dinner when Mum gets here. Bella, why don't you get Sam a snack? He probably shouldn't take these painkillers on an empty stomach.'

Bella gave Sam a grin as she said, 'Peanut butter on toast?' which I was guessing must be his favourite.

And as my sister walked past Dad she did something she hasn't done in a really long time. She threw her arms around him in a massive hug and said, 'Thanks for this, Dad. You're the best!'

After he'd eaten, Sam phoned and spoke to Bill, who agreed to fetch his bike.

'I could go with him and show him where it is,' I offered.

But Dad vetoed that instantly. 'You'll do no such thing.'

'I can go myself,' Sam said.

Dad just snorted. '*You'll* do no such thing either. You need to rest and keep that leg elevated as much as possible.'

'I'll be OK,' Sam said, and began to shuffle across the sofa bed as if to prove his point by standing up on his own.

'Hey, are you *trying* to get on my wrong side?' Dad snapped crossly.

Sam instantly stopped shuffling.

'You can draw a map for Bill,' Dad told him.

'It's in the middle of the woods,' Bella pointed out. 'There's nothing to draw, apart from trees.'

'Yeah,' Sam agreed. 'I'm not sure how easy it will be to find.'

'Then you'll just have to hope he doesn't charge you by the hour, won't you?' Dad said unsympathetically. 'Or you might end up having to *give* the bike to him – the part that doesn't belong to your uncle, that is.'

Sam flushed. 'You've spoken to Uncle John?'

'He phoned me again this morning. He's coming here next weekend to see you and collect the bike. Bill says he'll keep it at the garage until then.'

'So that's it? I don't even get a say?' Sam was scowling now for all he was worth.

Dad shrugged. 'I'd say I'm sorry, Sam, but we both know that's not true. Anyway, I think losing the bike is the least of your problems, judging by how angry your uncle sounded on the phone.'

When Aunt Thecla brought Grace home, my little sister was bouncing up and down with excitement. 'Aunt Thecla's bought two puppies!' she announced. 'We're going to get them as soon as they're old enough to leave their mother. And she says I can help name them!'

'Two?' I exclaimed. 'Wow!'

'Oh my God!' Dad declared. 'Isn't one bad enough?'

'Don't be such a killjoy, Paul,' Aunt Thecla snapped. 'They'll be good company for each other. Besides, we couldn't choose between them, could we, Grace?'

'Is Mummy upstairs?' Grace demanded. 'I want to tell her about the puppies.' And she immediately ran off.

'Libby, have you heard from Tansy today?' Aunt Thecla asked.

I shook my head.

'It's just, Michael told me she's decided to go back to Southampton to live with her mother.'

'When?' I asked.

'I'm not sure. In a few days I think.'

I nodded, trying to fight back the surge of disappointment I felt.

Just then we heard a yell and a loud clattering noise from the living room.

'Sam!' Bella exclaimed in alarm, following after Dad, who was charging to the rescue. Sam must have tried to get up on his own and lost his balance or something. He was sitting on the floor, having just knocked over the side table and sent everything on it flying. Fortunately his plaster cast still seemed to be in one piece.

He was red in the face as he murmured, 'I'm sorry. I just need to pee … use the bathroom, I mean … I didn't want to bother you.'

'Maybe you should get the boy a bucket,' Aunt Thecla suggested. 'It would be much easier for him.'

Sam looked like he wanted to disappear and Dad grinned as he handed him his crutches. 'Come on, son. Let's go.'

'Everything OK?' Mum asked as she joined us from upstairs. 'Goodness, this living room doesn't have a lot of space left when the sofa bed is out, does it?'

'It's going to be a tight fit having Sam living here with you,' Aunt Thecla said thoughtfully. 'I was just thinking, Nina, since I've got a perfectly good spare room, perhaps I could take him.'

Mum looked surprised. 'Are you serious, Thecla?'

'I wouldn't say it if I wasn't!'

'Mum, you can't do that to Sam!' Bella protested.

'Bella, don't be so rude,' Mum snapped. She gave our aunt a grateful smile. 'I must say, that's extremely kind of you.'

'I know how important Sam is to Bella.' As Bella gazed at her in disbelief Aunt Thecla added with a frown, 'Of course, he'd have to be well enough to get to the lavatory by himself first.'

Chapter Thirty-One

Over the next two days we somehow muddled through, with Dad helping Sam in lots of practical ways at home and Sam gradually relaxing enough to let him. He found himself on the receiving end of Dad's advice a lot, but the really weird thing was that he didn't seem to mind too much. It was almost as if he was relieved to be part of a family again.

Mum swung into mother-hen mode, buying Sam new clothes, making sure he ate properly and spending a lot of time talking to him about his own family and what he was hoping to do in the future. She actually brought home some of her dental instruments to give him a check-up since he hadn't had one in a while. He didn't seem to mind that too much either, and they even had a discussion about braces.

Aunt Thecla repeated her offer that Sam could stay with her and I knew it was something Mum and Dad were considering, although they both said it would have to wait until he didn't need as much practical help as he did at the moment.

Tansy had sent me some texts and left a message on my voicemail, but so far I hadn't got back to her. I was having trouble adjusting to the idea that she wasn't going to be starting at my new school with me. The thing was, I was beginning to feel nervous about St Clara's. I'm not very good at pushing myself forward in new social situations, and I was scared in case the other girls in my year had formed really tight friendship groups already. I suspected Tansy would have pushed enough for both of us if she'd been starting there with me. Now though, I was on my own ...

I suppose I felt sort of angry with her – a bit like she'd tricked me. It would have been different if she'd told me from the beginning that she might be going back to live with her mum. Then I wouldn't have got my hopes up so much. But she'd always been so adamant that she was staying here. It seemed to me that all she'd been doing was punishing her mum by making her beg sufficiently before agreeing to go home.

On my second day of ignoring Tansy's texts I walked into the living room as Dad was telling Sam what had happened to Murray. I stood quietly in the doorway, careful not to interrupt them, though I wasn't hiding the fact that I was there.

Sam said, 'That sounds awful. Seems like he was your mate and big brother rolled into one.'

'He was,' Dad said in a low voice.

There was a brief pause before Sam added quietly, 'I just want you to know that I'm a really careful driver and my bike's in really good nick, and I always wear the right gear and I make sure Bella does too.'

'I don't doubt that, Sam,' Dad said kindly, 'but it's not just your own driving you have to worry about, is it?'

'I know but …' Sam hesitated before continuing a little heatedly, 'but that's the same for everything! Driving a car, riding a pushbike, even just walking along the road.'

'Look, Sam,' Dad said, 'I can't argue with your logic, but frankly that still doesn't change how I feel about motorbikes.'

'Not even when you remember how much fun you had riding Murray's? You did have fun, didn't you?'

'I had a blast! Doesn't change how I feel about it now though.'

Sam let out an exasperated sigh. 'What kind of motorbike did Murray have, anyhow?'

'A Bantam – one of the late-Sixties models. The maximum speed they reached was fifty-seven miles per hour.' He looked at Sam as if he fully expected him to scoff at that.

'I guess that's all the speed you needed in the olden days,' he said with a cheeky grin. 'Actually, I know a bit about those old Bantams. My uncle bought one a couple of years ago as a restoration project. I used to help him with it. He sold it on eBay when it was finished.'

Listening to them was giving me an idea. But first I needed to speak to Tansy ...

I went to join Bella and Mum in the kitchen. Grace was round at Aunt Thecla's house getting another art lesson, and then they were going to the pet store in Castle Westbury to choose things for the puppies, who would be ready in two weeks' time.

'Look at this!' Bella was pointing to a house she'd spotted in the property pages of the local newspaper. 'It backs on to the woods with fields to one side, and it's got four bedrooms *and* a converted loft.'

'I'm not sure I like being so close to the woods,' Mum said. 'Though it's true the loft would make a good office for Dad.'

Dad's business was picking up, according to Bella, who'd told me he'd gained four new clients since we'd moved here. Not that I was meant to know there had ever been a problem. I made a mental note to use it to challenge Bella's theory that I was the only one in our family who ever got told what was going on.

'I'm going round to Tansy's,' I told them. 'I need to talk to her about something.'

'I thought you said you weren't going to bother with her now she's leaving,' Bella said.

'Oh, Libby, you didn't mean that, did you?' Mum said swiftly. 'I know you're disappointed she's not going to St Clara's with you, but you'll still get to see her when she comes back to visit her dad in the holidays. He's planning to buy a smaller place in the village, you know.'

'I really wanted her with me at school,' I said, quickly leaving the room before I sounded too emotional.

'You know Libby hasn't had a proper friend since Sarah left,' I heard Bella say in a concerned whisper. 'It's just such a shame that Tansy isn't staying.'

And I must say it felt weird hearing Bella talking about it to Mum like she was worried about me.

* * *

Tansy was in her front garden when I arrived at her house.

'Libby!' She sounded really pleased to see me. 'Why didn't you answer any of my texts? You do realise I'm leaving the day after tomorrow?'

'To go back to live with your mum,' I said. 'I know.' There was an awkward silence and I had to force myself to focus on the reason I'd come. 'Tansy, I came to ask if you could speak to your dad about something for me.'

'Of course,' she said without even waiting to hear what it was.

I told her my idea and she promised that if her dad agreed she would make sure he discussed it with Bill.

'Thanks.'

'Listen, I know I won't be at St Clara's with you,' she gushed, 'but we'll still be able to see each other whenever I come to stay with Dad.'

'Sure,' I answered stiffly.

'Dad's driving me back to Southampton on Saturday. Shall I pop in and say goodbye on our way out of the village?'

'We won't be in,' I said quickly. Mum had promised to take me and my sisters to Castle Westbury on Saturday. It was the day Sam's uncle was visiting to collect the

257

motorbike. Sam was dreading the confrontation, and he'd been really relieved when Dad had offered to stay and lend some support.

'Oh … well … I guess this is goodbye then,' Tansy mumbled, adding that she had a present for me – something else her dad had found when he'd been clearing out the garage. 'Your grandmother and mine were really good friends when they first lived next door to each other,' she told me. 'Dad found a photo of the two of them, so I got it framed for you.'

'For me?' I was a bit surprised.

'Yes, because honestly, Libby, your grandmother looks so like you in this photograph!' She shot me an excited grin. 'I'll go and get it.'

While I waited for her to come back, I braced myself for another round of how I was the spitting image of my big-boned, puffy-faced, thin-haired grandmother, who had died far too young and been missed far too much for me to object to the comparison.

Tansy returned with her gift and handed it to me. It was wrapped in purple paper and when I removed it and looked at the picture I thought at first that she must have made a mistake. It was a colour photograph and both young women in the picture were pretty. They looked to be in their early twenties and they were both smiling. Tansy's grandmother had long dark hair and she didn't look the least bit like Tansy. The other woman had long curly reddish hair – very similar to mine – glowing skin and pink cheeks with lots of freckles. She wore a red summer dress that showed off her curves and she had a red flower in her hair. She was laughing, looking like she didn't have a care in the world, and the two women had their arms around each other like they were the best of friends.

'Her name was Elisabeth too, wasn't it?' Tansy said.

I nodded, totally stunned. I realised I'd never seen a photograph of my grandmother when she was this young. 'She looks really different to the other photos I've seen,' I murmured. I gave Tansy a smile – the first genuine one I'd given her since I'd arrived that afternoon. 'Thank you.'

She smiled back. 'You're welcome.' She paused. 'I hope it goes OK for you at St Clara's. Oh … and by the way … when we took my uniform back to the shop Mrs Mayhew said there's another new girl starting in your year, so you won't be the only one …' She paused again. 'We can email and facetime each other if you want. And I'll see you at half-term when I come to visit Dad. We can still be friends, right?'

I nodded. 'Sure we can, Tansy.' And I gave her a hug.

Chapter Thirty-Two

A couple of days later Aunt Thecla came round so that we could tell Dad together about Murray's motorbike. She and Dad were on pretty friendly terms again. She'd told him where she'd really been that night when he was caught in the Godwin house, and she'd asked him to forgive her for lying to him. Dad hadn't talked about it afterwards – not to me at any rate – but at least I could be sure that he knew the truth now.

As I'd expected, Dad didn't jump up and down with enthusiasm straight away. In fact, he looked a bit dazed when he first heard that Murray's old bike had been found, and he couldn't seem to decide if he wanted to take a look at it or not.

Tansy's dad had done as I'd suggested and spoken to Bill about Sam. Bill had agreed that when Sam's leg was better he could restore the bike at his garage, and that he would supervise. All he asked was that Sam did some odd jobs about the place while he was there, and that Dad gave Bill first refusal if he decided to sell the bike after it was fully restored.

'If you two think I'm going to facilitate Sam building another motorbike then you must be a whole lot crazier than I thought!' Dad responded when we told him that.

'But, Paul, this isn't just any motorbike,' Aunt Thecla said softly. 'It's the one you rode with Murray.'

'Who died in a bike crash, remember?' Dad said.

'But not on *this* motorbike,' Aunt Thecla insisted firmly. 'Anyway, you don't have to keep it if you still feel that way at the end of the day. In any case, this will keep Sam occupied while Bella's at school. And if he and Bill get along, Bill says he'll take him on as his new apprentice when the boy he has now finishes at the end of the year.'

Dad sighed. I could tell Aunt Thecla's reasoning had got to him. 'Well, I suppose if the bike comes free and if it could lead to Sam having a job, then it might be worth considering. If Sam's up for it, that is.'

'Don't worry. He'll be up for it,' I said.

And of course Sam was.

* * *

I couldn't believe how soon the summer holiday ended and it was time for us to start the autumn term.

Mum drove all three of us to St Clara's on our first day.

At the senior school reception we found three other girls of differing ages standing around waiting. Mum left Bella and me on our own and dashed off to the junior department with Grace. Bella immediately started pacing up and down, looking bad-tempered and unfriendly. I knew it was just because she was nervous but I wished she'd stop. I tensed as our headmistress, Mrs McLusky, approached us.

'Good morning, girls,' she said in a calm voice. 'And welcome to St Clara's.'

Suddenly another girl burst in through the doors, looking flushed and anxious. 'Sorry I'm late,' she blurted, and I was totally shocked to see that it was Katie. She looked really different in her smart St Clara's uniform.

Mrs McLusky talked to us all in a very relaxed manner as she led us to our form rooms. I stayed close to Bella and made a point of not looking at Katie. What was she doing here when she'd said she went to school in Castle Westbury? I was starting to get a horrible panicky feeling.

What if she turned all the other girls against me? What if I got too nervous to stand up for myself and they all laughed at me? I felt tears prick my eyes and I had to remind myself what Mum had told me last night when she'd spotted how nervous I was getting: 'Just be yourself, Libby. That's good enough!' The trouble was, I *so* badly wanted to fit in here.

When Mrs McLusky stopped to show one of the other girls to her form room, I turned to Katie and blurted, 'How come *you're* here?' It came out a lot more awkwardly than I'd intended.

Katie answered me a bit warily. 'Mum and Dad wanted to send me here before, but they couldn't afford it. Now my dad's got a new job, so they can. I didn't know I had a place here until last week. Someone who was meant to be starting dropped out.'

Bella was looking at us curiously 'You two know each other?'

'A little,' Katie said politely.

I nodded, trying not to blame Katie for being here when Tansy wasn't.

'So what did your pals say about it?' I asked a little sharply.

She pulled a face. 'I haven't told them yet. I guess

263

they'll find out when they get to school.' She paused. 'I'm sorry they weren't very friendly to you before.'

'All right, girls,' Mrs McLusky said as she rejoined us. 'Katie and Libby, your classroom is next.'

I glanced at Katie, who was nervously chewing her bottom lip. Maybe she wasn't looking to make trouble for me after all. Maybe, like me, she just wanted to fit in.

I caught Bella's eye as we prepared to go our separate ways. I could see she was feeling really tense – worse than me, in fact. I can't say I blamed her.

'See you at break?' I asked, deliberately making it a question because I remembered how she'd never liked to be seen with me at our last school. 'I promise I'll try not to embarrass you by being too dorky,' I added with a smile.

She smiled back. 'Don't be daft – I'm *glad* you're here!'

'You'll be fine, Bella,' I told her. 'Just be yourself and everyone will like you.' I had a flashback then to a time long ago when I was the one who was scared to go to school and she was the one who took charge. I wondered if she was remembering that too. Judging by the sparkle in her eyes, I think maybe she was.

I felt strangely brave and calm as I stepped into my new classroom. I even felt a tiny bit excited. After all, I was Libby. I could do this.

ALL ABOUT GWYNETH!

If you'd like to find out more about Gwyneth Rees,
check out her author page on
Facebook.com/GwynethReesAuthor
or email her on **gwyneth.rees@bloomsbury.com**.

Please make sure you that you have permission from a parent or guardian.

Look out for more fantastic books by
GWYNETH REES!

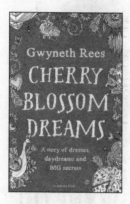